KV-010-070

SPECIAL MESSAGE TO READERS

This book is published under the auspices of

THE ULVERSCROFT FOUNDATION
(registered charity No. 264873 UK)

Established in 1972 to provide funds for research, diagnosis and treatment of eye diseases. Examples of contributions made are: —

A Children's Assessment Unit at Moorfield's Hospital, London.

•

Twin operating theatres at the Western Ophthalmic Hospital, London.

•

A Chair of Ophthalmology at the Royal Australian College of Ophthalmologists.

•

The Ulverscroft Children's Eye Unit at the Great Ormond Street Hospital For Sick Children, London.

You can help further the work of the Foundation by making a donation or leaving a legacy. Every contribution, no matter how small, is received with gratitude. Please write for details to:

THE ULVERSCROFT FOUNDATION,
The Green, Bradgate Road, Anstey,
Leicester LE7 7FU, England.
Telephone: (0116) 236 4325

In Australia write to:
THE ULVERSCROFT FOUNDATION,
c/o The Royal Australian College of
Ophthalmologists,
27, Commonwealth Street, Sydney,
N.S.W. 2010.

Rona Randall was born in Cheshire, though her parents moved to London soon afterwards. She won a scholarship to a College of Art, but her parents regarded it as too precarious a career and insisted that she did secretarial training instead. She rebelled against this eventually and became a drama student, went into rep., and understudied in London. Later, however, she became secretary to the editor of *Woman's Journal* and began writing seriously in her spare time. She has now published over 40 novels as well as more than 100 short stories and a non-fiction book on Jordon and the Holy Land which has a foreword by King Hussein.

Rona Randall is married with one son, also married, and lives in Sussex. She lists her hobbies as antiques, the theatre and travel.

THE FROZEN CEILING

When Tessa Pickard found the note amongst her father's possessions, instinct told her that *this* had been responsible for his suicide, not the professional disgrace which had ruined his career as a mountaineer and instructor. The note was cryptic, anonymous, and bore a Norwegian postmark. Tessa promptly set out for Norway, determined to trace the anonymous letter-writer, but unprepared for the drama she was to uncover — or that compelling Max Hyerdal, whom she met on board a Norwegian ship, was to change her whole life.

Books by Rona Randall
Published by The House of Ulverscroft:

THE DRAYTON LEGACY
THE POTTER'S NIECE
THE RIVAL POTTERS
ARROGANT DUKE
CURTAIN CALL
KNIGHT'S KEEP
GLENRANNOCH
THE LADIES OF HANOVER SQUARE
THE WATCHMAN'S STONE
MOUNTAIN OF FEAR
THE EAGLE AT THE GATE
SEVEN DAYS FROM MIDNIGHT
DRAGONMEDE
LYONHURST

RONA RANDALL

THE FROZEN CEILING

Complete and Unabridged

ULVERSCROFT
Leicester

Originally published under the title of
'Silent Thunder'

First Large Print Edition
published 1999

British Library CIP Data

Randall, Rona
    The frozen ceiling.—Large print ed.—
Ulverscroft large print series: romance
1. Love stories
2. Large type books
I. Title
823.9'14 [F]

ISBN 0–7089–4062–5

Published by
F. A. Thorpe (Publishing) Ltd.
Anstey, Leicestershire
Set by Words & Graphics Ltd.
Anstey, Leicestershire
Printed and bound in Great Britain by
T. J. International Ltd., Padstow, Cornwall

This book is printed on acid-free paper

1

Coming across the letter amongst her father's possessions was a shock, not because of what it said, which seemed meaningless, but because he had locked it away, thus proving it was not. A thing had to be important for a man like James Pickard to keep it. He had never been a hoarder, except of things necessary to his work: notes for lectures or broadcasts or articles or books, all meticulously docketed because that was the kind of man he was, a well-organised man with no room in his life for clutter and certainly no room for unsigned scraps of paper bearing meaningless questions. Once a scribbled reminder had been dealt with it would be torn from his note pad and thrown away, another detail disposed of. 'And now let's get on with the next.' That had been James. He liked, and was accustomed to, space. A clear desk. Open country. Wide bare peaks exposed to the sky. Never a man of secrets and therefore never the type to lock away unsigned notes written in an unknown hand by some unknown person in an unknown land.

But there it was, staring up at her, a brief question written smoothly in English. '*Do you remember the Jostedal Glacier?*' Just that and no more, but it held the sickening thrust of all anonymous letters.

She turned the envelope over and stared again at the Norwegian stamp with the postmark which was already imprinted on her mind — *Vijne, Norge*. The date stood out clearly, adding to the uneasiness which had at first been vague and was now as sharp as a nagging tooth. That date was significant. Ten days after all the press publicity, two days before James Pickard's death.

And he had kept the note. He had shown it to no one. Hiding it from the world proved that the question was significant and important, the absence of a signature adding a touch of menace. The more she stared at it the more convinced she became that this was not something to be ignored; she couldn't tear it up, throw it away, forget it. For some reason it had mattered to her father, and she had to find out why, who had sent it, and whether it had anything to do with his suicide.

He just wasn't the type to take his life without reason, and although his action had been attributed to the shock of young Peter Wynyard's death and the slur it had cast upon his name, nothing would ever convince his daughter that the cause was not greater than that. Tessa knew her father well. She had been his right hand, dealing with the administrative side of his famous climbing school so that he was free to devote himself to his work and his pupils. That devotion had been a real and genuine thing, which was another reason why public opinion following the coroner's enquiry had been unfair. People quickly mistrusted a man who let an inexperienced climber go out alone and it took only one such case to point an accusing finger. People believed what they wanted to believe, laid blame where they wanted to blame. A man who ran a climbing school was responsible for the safety of his pupils, and one as well known as James Pickard was a fine target.

It made little difference, although some sections of the Press had been fair enough to mention it, that the school's good record had been quoted at the enquiry, along with Pickard's distinguished career and his war service with the Snow Corps in Norway. The fact remained that a boy had been allowed to go out alone, and as a result had fallen to his death. It also made little difference that young Wynyard had been headstrong, chafing against restrictions, ignoring the rules of mountaineering which stipulated that no inexperienced climber, or even an experienced one, should go climbing solo without leaving a note of the time of his departure and the direction he had taken. It had been Saturday, and a group had gone dancing in Keswick. It was assumed that Wynyard was with them, hence the delay in sending out a search party. Death by misadventure had been the verdict, but gossip and disapproval had done their worst.

Tessa folded the note carefully and replaced it in the envelope. Could this thin sheet of airmail paper have been the final arrow-thrust to send her father over the edge of despair, and, if so, why? It was a remorseless question which refused to be silenced. She could not only hear the words of the letter echoing in her brain, but see them reflected through the envelope — taunting, prodding, reminding, insinuating. But insinuating what? Why should James Pickard remember the Jostedal Glacier, and where was it, anyway?

The thought released the first essential action, a swift movement from his desk to his bookshelves, stacked with maps and files and meticulous records of climbing routes all over Europe and beyond. He had led expeditions as far away as the Himalayas and

4

Mexico, and nearer home in parts of Europe and Asia. There was hardly a mountainous country in which he had not climbed and certainly no mountainous area which was not carefully mapped. She ran her fingers along the alphabetically arranged shelves, finally settling on N. To her surprise, there was little on Norway, no more than a volume or two compared with at least a dozen or more on other places.

But James had loved Norway. Although he had rarely spoken of his service days there with an Allied mountain regiment, his love of the country had communicated itself to his daughter — and perhaps to Ruth as well. Was that why she always looked bored when he referred to the place? But Ruth had been bored by everything connected with climbing, hating the school and the wild isolation of it. Tessa couldn't remember when she had first become aware of her father's unhappiness and her mother's discontent.

The door opened, admitting a faint but unmistakable whiff of Chanel, and without turning Tessa knew that her mother had entered. This perfume travelled before Ruth like an introductory theme song and it characterised her whole personality — elegant, cloying, indulged.

'So there you are!' The voice was petulant,

as always. 'I might have known you'd be cooped up in *his* room.'

'Someone has to go through his things,' Tessa answered steadily, and opened a Norwegian atlas at random, flicking the pages until reaching the index. A . . . *Ae* . . . *Aeb* . . . The pages spun like leaves until they reached J. *Ja* . . . *Jae* . . . *Jaed* . . .

'There's Dan. Why can't he go through them?' Ruth asked.

'He's not one of the family.'

'But he's going to be. I can't pretend I'm not sorry in a way, nice as he is and certainly handsome, but one climber in the family has been more than enough.'

The atlas slammed shut. Tessa turned and faced her mother. The elegant black dress seemed a mockery, worn by someone playing at mourning. The whole business had been nothing but humiliation to Ruth, never grief. 'How could he *do* it to me?' she had wailed. 'The shame of it! As if I hadn't endured enough through that dreadful public enquiry without the disgrace of suicide to follow!'

Any minute now the self-pitying tirade would pour out again. (*And if it does, I shall scream, I shall scream, I shall scream!*)

Mercifully, it didn't. Instead, with that feckless change of mood which Ruth could switch on and off at will, she smiled tearfully

6

and said, 'Darling, what would I do without you? You're a tower of strength.' A helpless gesture, a vague flutter of a lace edged handkerchief, another whiff of Chanel. 'I really am glad you're not so sensitive as I. You'll never know what it's like to suffer — truly suffer. I mean — look at your dress! It's unfeeling, to say the least. Surely something a little quieter . . . '

'Father would have hated it. He liked me in bright colours. He said all young people should wear bright colours, always.'

She took the atlas back to the big desk and spread it out, willing her mother to go away, shutting her ears to the empty voice, but defenceless against the flow of words.

'I've been thinking, darling, that I really ought to get away. Rest. Sea air. Peace. I need so desperately to find peace . . . '

Then find it. For God's sake go and find it, Tessa thought in silent desperation. You went in search of it while the enquiry was on. You ran away. You deserted him. You hid in some smug South Coast hotel while he faced up to things alone. *Suffer?* It was he who suffered. And I, and I . . .

J. *Ja* . . . *Jae* . . . *Jaed* . . . The pages spun to *Jo* . . . *Jod* . . . *Joef* . . . *Jos* . . .

'You might at least listen, Tessa.'

'I am listening. You need rest. You need

peace. Funny, you were always complaining that this place was too peaceful, even when the school was full.'

Ruth shuddered. 'Darling, don't remind me of those days. I want to forget them. I want to forget all those hearty young men and strapping young women clumping around in heavy boots and hideous gear. What *is* that book?'

'An atlas. Yes, I agree, Mother. I understand. You can get away, surely? What is there to stop you? You're well provided for — Father made sure of that. The lawyers will settle everything and I can deal with his personal things. I'd like to.'

Ruth gave a sigh which was half relief and half distaste. 'Morbid, that's what you are, Tessa. I actually believe you enjoy the job.'

She didn't answer. She couldn't. She was staring at a name in the index — *Jostedal, Page 5, square A/D*. And then she was leafing backwards through the book; the room, her mother, everything else forgotten. And there it was, an area high above the Fjaerland Fjord, a vast space clearly marked Jostedal Glacier. And leaping out, to the right of the village of Fjaerland, another name — so small that had it not been stamped indelibly upon her mind Tessa would never have noticed it.

Vijne.

A dot on a map. A hamlet, no more. An isolated corner deep in the heart of fjord country. She raced to the Glossary: '*Vijne, pop. 300. Altitude 450'. A low-lying village at the apex of the Fjaerland Fjord.*' No more than that. There was, apparently, nothing more worth mentioning.

She didn't hear Ruth leave the room. She heard nothing until a crash from outside brought her head up with a jerk. The desk faced tall french windows which, in turn, faced a wide drive. At the foot of the drive stood a lorry, and a couple of men were about to haul something on to it — a large board which had stood beside the gates ever since James Pickard set up his school after the war.

She was through the windows in a flash and pelting down the drive, shouting at them to stop. The men paused and stared, the board with its large gilt letters turned blindly towards the sky, waiting to be hauled to its death.

'What are you doing? Who told you to take that down? Put it back, *put it back!*'

The men continued to stare, dumb and bewildered, and a voice said, 'Tessa my dear, pull yourself together. *I* told them to take it away. Someone had to, and I wanted to spare you a painful task.'

'Dan! Dan, how *could* you?'

'Darling,' he said gently, 'it has to come down, but it isn't going to be destroyed, merely repainted.'

She was sobbing. He put an arm round her and nodded to the men quietly. The gesture was characteristic of Dan Delaney; he was a quiet and thorough man who never put a foot wrong, even when climbing. Especially when climbing. That was why he was one of the best instructors her father had ever employed. James had never had anything but praise for him, even though in some subtle way Tessa had always felt he was careful to avoid anything else. For her sake? Because he knew she loved Dan?

The school sign moved again as the men hauled it on to the lorry.

'Put it back,' Tessa ordered.

'Now, darling, be reasonable . . . '

'*Put it back.*'

One man looked at the other, raised his eyebrows, and shrugged expressively. The other looked at the girl, compassion in his rugged face. 'Hold it,' he said. 'Hold it, mate.'

Dan's normally patient voice held a testy note. 'Tessa, I know you're overwrought and you've been through a bad time, but the school is closed. You've got to accept that fact.'

'Then why send the board to be repainted?'

'Because when we reopen it will need a new name. And you know we're going to reopen together.'

'Then the board can stay up until we do.'

'But not,' he said, 'with that name on it.'

Within the pockets of her jacket her hands clenched slowly, one closing over a thin airmail letter which rustled beneath her touch.

'And what name do you propose to substitute?' she asked stonily.

'We can talk about that later.'

'No. Now. Not that there's anything to discuss because this school has only ever had one name and always will. It's the Pickard Climbing School. That's the name on the board and the name that's going to remain in memory of the man who founded it, so put it back, please. Right away. At present it can only be moved by my authority, and I don't give it.'

She turned and walked back to the house, ignoring Dan's footsteps behind her. Once inside her father's study she turned and faced him. Over his shoulder she could see the

11

length of the drive and the men re-erecting the school sign.

Dan's determined face was flushed.

'Did you *have* to humiliate me in front of those men?'

'You sound like Mother. She's talked an awful lot about humiliation lately. Anyway, you haven't the right, as yet, to decide on what shall and shall not be done about the school.'

'Your father left me a share.'

'In the event of our marrying — yes. If we don't, you receive a substantial sum in appreciation of your help as . . . '

'As his right hand. As assistant principal. As his natural successor. And, darling, we *are* going to be married.'

He put his arms round her and held her close. 'You're tired,' he said. 'Just leave things to me.'

She drew away.

'I'll have to, for a while. I'm going away and I'm not sure when I'll be back. Mother's going away too, so there'll be precious little to do here until my father's estate is settled.'

'That's a good idea — your going away, I mean. You need a complete change. I'll miss you, of course, but you're on the edge of cracking. Take a holiday and don't worry about a thing.'

12

'I won't. I'll leave it all to the lawyers. That's their job — to do the worrying and the arranging and issuing orders on my behalf when necessary. We're not married yet, Dan.'

She didn't mean it to sound like a rebuff. As Dan said, she was tired and on the edge of cracking. She put a hand upon his arm placatingly.

'The board stays up — promise?'

'Of course I promise. What else can I do? As you point out, we're not married yet.'

He was hurt, and she knew it, and could do nothing about it. His action had been a thoughtful one, planned to spare her. That it had only succeeded in making her suffer was something he could not have anticipated. She felt ashamed, but at the same time apprehensive. If a man who loved a girl was insensitive to the things which mattered most in her life, what sort of a marriage would they have?

'Where do you plan to go, Tessa?'

'Somewhere I've never been before. Norway.'

'Norway! My dear girl, you should get away to the sun.'

'It can shine in Norway too.'

'Well,' he said briskly, 'it's good climbing country. Be sure to pack your kit.'

Quite suddenly, hysterically, she wanted to laugh. Above everything and before everything, Dan was a climber. James Pickard had been a climber too, but not absorbed in it to the point of insensitivity.

2

The entranc e to the fjord was bigger than she expected, the mountains more vast, the whole scene more spectacular, but this was Viking country; a land of snowcapped peaks and glaciers, of trolls and legends and fables, of hunters and climbers, skiers and adventurers. A land of strength and incredible beauty.

For the first time she felt a stirring of life beneath the numbness which had lingered since her father's death. She had actually arrived. She was sailing at last towards the Sojne Fjord, and beyond that to Fjaerland, every throb of the *Valkyrie*'s engines bringing her nearer to her goal — the remote source of the anonymous letter. Without even opening her handbag to glance inside she could see the now familiar envelope, worn with too much handling, and the taunting, worrying, silent question which seemed to hold the venom of a viper. Was that why they were called poison-pen letters, these cowardly unsigned notes written by cowardly unseen people?

Rain spattered down as the small cargo ship plied its way between the scattered islands which marked the Norwegian coast; tiny outcrops of rocky scrub rising from the sea like wild gardens. All the way from Bergen, where she had come aboard, these projections straggled northwards to Trondheim, the Lofoten Islands, and the North Cape, but the *Valkyrie* turned off into the Sojne Fjord which penetrated for a hundred miles into the heart of western Norway, a bastioned stronghold of water as deep as the surrounding mountains were high.

A voice startled her. 'Don't take this as a sample of our weather. It always rains at the mouth of the Sojne. We do get sun, even up there where the snow lies.'

A man had paused beside her, pointing to the towering pinnacles above, hand out-thrust from the sleeve of a thick nautical sweater knitted in oiled wool and vividly patterned in Norwegian design. Right now it was covered with oilskins, but the cuff protruded and she recognised it. It belonged to the man who had sat near her at lunch. Meals were served at one long table in the ship's saloon and he had been at the head. Tessa had noticed his lean, hewn sort of face reluctantly, vaguely resentful of the way in which he had scrutinised her, as if summing her up. Finally she had put an end to it by

16

cutting the rest of the meal and returning to her cabin. She was in no mood for talking to strangers these days, particularly strangers she was never likely to meet again.

For this reason she had come aboard after dinner the night before and breakfasted in her cabin this morning. The cargo ship was due to reach Balestrand this evening, when the few passengers it carried would go their separate ways, she would go hers, and this craggy-featured sailor would do likewise. She wouldn't be sorry. There was a compelling quality about him which she wanted to analyse, but was stubbornly determined not to.

It had been comparatively easy to ignore him at lunch, leaving the passengers to carry the conversation while she opted out of it, but it wasn't so easy when a man came up to you and spoke directly. Courtesy was an effort, but she clutched at it and made some comment about the fantastic scenery being like a jumbo edition of the Highlands and Lochs of Scotland. 'Twice as big and twice as vast.'

'You come from Scotland?' His English was fluent, only inflection and precision betraying that it was not his native tongue.

'No. From England.'

He acknowledged this with a monosyllabic

sound which might have indicated indifference or disappointment. She couldn't be sure and wasn't interested enough to find out. She was still tightly enclosed in a defensive shell and unwilling to be prised out of it. It was a shell of numbness and anger and fear and bewilderment, shot through with a vein of menace which emanated like a tangled skein from the anonymous letter. Right from that moment, the moment when she had found it and read it and stared at it blankly, this thread of fear had begun to stir, increasing from bewilderment to confusion, from confusion to alarm, growing insidiously in her mind until now it was interwoven with every thought and emotion; a kind of strangulating grip like the tentacles of an octopus from which she couldn't shake free, and from which she never would shake free until she tracked down the writer and wrested the truth out of him.

As secretly as it had lain hidden in her handbag, so it had remained in her mind. She had told no one about it, not even Dan, although he had been her most intimate confidant for the past two years. It was Dan who had gradually interposed between her father and herself, making her aware that she was a woman, not merely a girl; something more mature than the devoted daughter of a famous man. And James had looked on, seeing what was happening and knowing that it had to happen, and that he was glad.

There had been nothing possessive in her father's love for her and if he admired Dan more as a climber than as a person he never said so, never hinted, never displayed any disappointment in her choice. It was only after his death that she remembered little things, uneasy or sudden questions. 'Are you sure, my dear? Really sure? Because it's not too late to turn back, or to admit a mistake.' Things like that would be said casually, without premeditation. Or so it seemed. And so they had been forgotten, or failed to register with any degree of significance. Not until after his death had they begun to return like echoes in her mind, making her wonder why he had said them and why she only remembered them now.

Unlike Ruth, Dan had been a tower of strength both during and after the Wynyard affair, taking over the running of the school and studiously maintaining discipline as well as quenching gossip. James Pickard could not have had a more loyal ally and Dan deserved the reward of a half-share in the school. Ruth was glad to be rid of it, more than content with the comfortable annuity left to her and the ample trust which yielded an income guaranteed to cushion her against discomfort for the rest of her life.

Looking back now, Tessa wondered why she had not confided in Dan, of all people. He was the obvious person, the only one to whom she could have shown the anonymous note and expressed her fears. Her silence now seemed inexplicable. She loved him, didn't she? She trusted him? She hadn't withheld the letter simply because of that distressing little incident concerning the school sign and because it had made her feel, quite wrongly, that he had been jumping the gun a bit, eager to see his own name replacing Pickard's?

Or had her silence been due to the knowledge that Dan would have urged her to tear the thing up and forget it? That was the sort of practical advice he would have handed out because he was not emotionally involved, and which she would have refused to heed because she was. This explanation was more satisfactory than the first, so she settled for it, resolving to write and tell him about the letter sometime — but not yet.

'Something on your mind?' the Norwegian asked. 'I noticed it at lunch. Your withdrawal, I mean.'

She jerked to awareness, instantly defensive. She had faced enough probing and interrogation back home in England; she'd

20

be damned if she would face it in a foreign country from a man she didn't know and didn't want to know.

'Nothing,' she answered shortly, and turned away.

His hand shot out and caught her wrist. 'I don't believe you,' he said.

She tried to wrench free, and failed. 'Let me *go*. What right have you to lay hands on me?'

'None whatever.' His voice was bland, undercut by laughter. 'I'm curious, that's all, and if I let you go my curiosity will be unsatisfied. Apart from that, I'm a man who likes to get his own way.'

'With everything, or with women in particular?'

'Women in particular, but I have a damn good try for everything.'

She could believe it — the bold eyes and hard mouth spoke for themselves. She gave a sudden jerk and her wrist was free. Surprise caught her off balance, making her clutch the ship's rail to steady herself, and the moment cheated her of the opportunity to make a getaway. It also gave him the opportunity to say, 'What's made you so defensive? You're prickly as a porcupine. It isn't just shyness, I'm sure of that, so why do you want to run away? I'm not intent on seduction, and if I were this deck wouldn't be the ideal place.' His voice and his eyes were laughing.

She answered coldly, 'If you were, I would know how to handle the situation.'

'I can tell that. That's why I don't understand you. Why did you come aboard so late and why go straight to your cabin and remain there? You only emerged for lunch today and then cleared off in an almighty hurry. You didn't want to talk to anyone. You don't now. Particularly to me. Why did you come aboard so late?' he repeated.

'I scarcely had time to catch the ship.'

'That's not true. You crossed from England . . . '

She jerked in surprise. 'How do you know?'

'It's a natural assumption. You bought your ticket at Bergen shortly after the ship from Newcastle docked, a full two hours before we sailed. Besides, the booking list was sent aboard in advance, so that cabins could be allocated. That's how I know just when you made your reservation and that you had plenty of time to come aboard for dinner.'

'Perhaps I wanted to see something of Bergen.'

'In the dark? It isn't the sort of place for a young woman to wander alone in, and you're not the sort to do so.'

He was certainly perceptive.

'You must be Tessa Richard, Cabin B,' he continued. 'How do I know? Because you're the only English passenger aboard and because I'm skipper, purser, everything but cook on this vessel. It's a family line, and I run it.'

She wasn't interested, and showed it, hoping to deflate him. She didn't even bother to put him right about her surname. She had noticed the mistake on her boarding card, a confusion made by the ticket clerk at Bergen, which she hadn't bothered to correct because the man's English was stilted and, as now, she had been in no mood for talking to strangers. All she had wanted was to be alone, and this had been achieved by eating a solitary meal in a quiet restaurant where the service had proved to be so slow that she had barely ten minutes in which to get aboard the *Valkyrie*.

'What on earth did you do with yourself during those two hours?' the man asked.

She answered abruptly, 'You're too inquisitive.'

'Aren't I?'

'And apparently incapable of being snubbed.'

'Totally.'

Unexpectedly, she wanted to laugh. She

could feel it quivering inside her and it was so long since she had felt that way that she was taken by surprise, and even more surprised that such a man as this could be responsible. She could feel her mouth tilting at the corners and in order to check a response which she knew would please him she said at random, 'You speak English well.'

'Most Norwegians do. It's a second language with us. I also happened to have English grandparents on my mother's side. Not that I ever saw much of them. They went back to England when I was a kid and both are dead now.'

There was a note of indifference in his voice, but she made no comment, and as it turned out none was necessary.

'You're right,' he said. 'I've never grieved for them. Don't look so surprised — your face is a dead give-away. You were wondering why I sound uncaring about my English grandparents, but how else can I feel about people I can scarcely remember and hardly knew? Apart from that, I happen to think the world of my father, who is Norwegian, and if you think there's an implication there, you could be right.'

'The implication being that you don't like the British. In that case, I'll spare you the unpleasantness of talking to me, and myself the unpleasantness of listening to you.'

This time she did turn away, walking the length of the deck in order to put as much distance as possible between them. Finding a secluded corner in the stern she let her glance roam up the mountains, sliver-sliced with waterfalls racing down to join the fjord. The wild North Sea had been left behind and now the mountains rose like precipices from the water, closer and closer so that torrent and cascade echoed loudly. It was like the back-drop for some spectacular musical, with Grieg as composer. At any moment she expected to see Peer Gynt come riding down the mountainside on his reindeer, or hear Solveig's song echoing across the water. The wild beauty of it all was calming and she was able to dismiss the unlikable Norwegian until his step sounded nearby, stopping again at her side and forcing her to look up.

'Do you climb?' he asked. 'If not, you will have to learn. I will teach you.'

'Thanks,' she said laconically. There was little he could teach her in that line, if he did but know. She had had the finest instructor from the time she owned her first pair of climbing boots.

'Is that all you have to say? I was hoping for more.'

That was a leading remark to which she refused to rise. If he wanted to start an affair, he could look elsewhere. She fumbled in her bag for cigarettes and the anonymous letter rustled as her fingers brushed against it. The sound and the contact immediately made this man seem unimportant. She had other things on her mind.

His hand flicked a lighter and held it towards her, touching her cigarette. She gave a nod of thanks and replaced the packet in her handbag, deliberately with-holding the slightest encouragement to stay. He smiled and took out his own, impervious to either hint or snub.

'I mean it,' he said. 'I would like to teach you.'

'There'll be neither the time nor the opportunity.'

'We'll make both. You're going to Balestrand. That suits me well. I live close by.'

She suppressed a smile, pleased because he was wrong.

'Well, anyway, your ticket goes to Balestrand. I've checked.'

She thought wryly that if he hoped to date her, he was optimistic. She had little time in which to trace the writer of the anonymous letter, which might have been posted far from the writer's home in any case. She knew that was a frequent cover-up, a coward's way of dodging discovery. So Vijne might be a wrong lead and for all she knew she might be chasing a red herring. Unfortunately it was the only herring she had to chase.

She still didn't want to talk to the skipper, but was compelled to because he lingered. She said at random, 'If you love mountains so much, why leave them for the sea?'

'I've told you — this shipping line is the family business. My father can't run it any more, so I have to. For that reason I came back home.'

'From where?'

'Roaming the world. I've been just about everywhere and done just about everything.'

She could believe that — he looked the type — but because she didn't want to hear his life story she turned a discouraging ear and gave herself up to enjoying her cigarette, leaning back against the bulkhead and closing her eyes, but her withdrawal failed to silence him.

'I'm not sorry,' he continued. 'This is a good life, but one thing beats it. Climbing.'

She might have known. In Norway just about everybody climbed, or ski-ed, or both. It was part of their life; in some regions, a necessary part. She had always known

27

that she herself would never make a great climber or even a wildly enthusiastic one, but she had stuck at it for her father's sake, wanting to compensate for Ruth's ill-concealed boredom. Even his writing had failed to interest his wife. She had merely resented the hours it compelled him to spend in his study, turning out books and articles and radio talks which had helped to establish not only his name but his climbing school as well. Not for the first time Tessa wondered why such an ill-matched pair had married.

The Norwegian asked suddenly, 'What made you choose a cargo boat instead of the fjord steamer? You would have travelled more luxuriously.'

She gave up, and opened her eyes. 'No doubt, but at greater expense. Anyway, I'm very comfortable and by travelling slowly I can see the fjord country.'

'I'll show you more. From Balestrand I'll take you to Flaam, right at the tip of the Sojne.'

'Sorry. I'll be too busy.'

He shrugged, then pointed ahead. 'We're coming in to Lavik. We'll stay there for about an hour, taking a load aboard. If you go ashore don't wander far, because the next cargo boat won't be along for two days.'

'I think I'll stay aboard.'

'In solitude? It's what you want, isn't it? You have prickly emotional antennae that come waving out at me. You dislike me, I know.' He shrugged again and headed towards a companionway.

'It's mutual, isn't it?' she said to his retreating back. 'You made it plain enough that you dislike the British.'

He turned, fixing her with a hard glance. 'Not all, Miss Richard. Just one in particular.'

She knew what he meant by that. It was her turn to shrug.

3

The cargo boat took twenty-four hours to do a journey which the luxury fjord steamers covered in considerably less, but the trip offered greater interest at far less cost, apart from which Tessa wanted greater solitude than the crowded steamer offered. The leisurely approach also initiated her into this strange new world in a way which no rushed arrival would have afforded, slowly introducing her to the locale which her father had known and loved, and from which the disturbing reminder from the past had come.

Although she had set herself a time limit of two months in which to trace the letter-writer, some instinct urged her to arrive by the slow route, because in so doing she could savour the atmosphere and the people who created it. So although she sought solitude she spent it on deck, watching the fjord villages pass by and studying the people as they came aboard or departed, sometimes going ashore herself whenever the vessel stayed long enough.

It was magnificent country, sometimes

intimidating when the sheer sides of mountains pressed closer and closer, rising straight from the water and disappearing into mist-enshrouded skies above, wild bastions enclosing the world within the hollow of their giant hands, and dwarfing the cargo vessel until, midget-like, she was no more than a fly hovering upon the surface of the fjord, a speck crawling into the unknown; then suddenly the gigantic walls would recede and the mountain mists with them, unveiling the fjord in all its splendour.

Once Lavik was left behind, the zigzag course began; from Tredal to Vikum, from Vikum to Vadheim, stopping at each place to unload passengers and cargo, and taking more aboard. Sheep, goats, and cattle were slung in hammocks from the hold on to the quay, village people embarked and disembarked, using the cargo boat as they would a bus to get from hamlet to hamlet; hikers and climbers shed their kit on deck and went below to the small dining saloon where food was perpetually available. The natives appeared to be stolid, pleasant, practical people accepting the wild conditions of their lives unemotionally, and from their clear-eyed honest faces it was impossible to imagine such a breed producing anything so devious as an anonymous letter-writer.

Time seemed to have little meaning; no one worried when the scheduled departure from each port of call was delayed by unexpected additions to the cargo, with the result that arrival at Balestrand was late by more than an hour. By then evening was far advanced, and as the *Valkyrie* emerged from the winding confines of the fjord into the vast expanse of water which marked the widest stretch of the Sojne, the whole area was bathed in flames of setting sun. The mountains had receded, providing a backdrop of purple peaks silhouetted against a vivid sky, the waters gold-tipped.

Balestrand itself nestled upon a tongue of land which marked the junction of the Sojne with the Fjaerland Fjord — a narrow strip of water which wound like a green ribbon to Fjaerland and eventually to all-important, significant Vijne. From this division of the waters the mainstream of the Sojne continued on its course to Aurland until its final culmination at Flaam.

The travel agent's itinerary instructed Tessa to terminate her voyage at Balestrand, from where she would be met by an hotel launch from the Nordfjord Hotel at Fjaèrland, but she didn't have to go in search of the craft because no sooner had the *Valkyrie* tied up and her gangway been lowered than a young man came striding aboard, tall and blond and athletic. Even in her present emotional state Tessa couldn't fail to notice him, for apart from being good-looking there was an amiable goodwill about him which caught the eye. Here was no complicated personality, no ruthless man intent upon getting his own way or capable of nursing strong prejudices.

She liked the look of him and was surprised when he stopped before her and said, 'You must be Tessa Pickard — you're the only one who looks English enough. My name's Hatton — Steve Hatton — from the Nordfjord Hotel. I was asked to meet you because we're fellow-countrymen, also because Olaf couldn't be spared. He runs the hotel launches, but he's had to go to Flaam to pick up other guests. These your bags? Then let's get weaving, shall we?'

Tessa was glad to; equally glad to leave the *Valkyrie* and the disturbing skipper, although he had given her a wide berth since their antagonistic encounter. He wasn't the type to accept dismissal by a woman, so it wasn't surprising that he disliked her. Tessa followed Steve Hatton on to the quayside without a backward glance.

'I didn't expect to be met, especially by an Englishman,' she said as they headed towards the mouth of Fjaerland Fjord. 'What brought you to Norway?'

'Sheer love of the place. I used to work for a sports journal in England; now I freelance, spending most of the year in this country. It was one of those things which just happened. The leading sports writer met with an accident and couldn't cover the winter Olympics at Holmenkollen — that's the famous ski-jump outside Oslo — so I was sent instead, which was a break for me because I not only got in some ski-ing myself but had the chance of a job as seasonal instructor, based at Voss. Who wouldn't snap up a chance like that? So when I returned to London I handed in the reporting job and hared back here fast. In the summer I teach fishing and sailing in the fjords. I began in the Hardanger, then the Sojne, and now I've been lured to this new hotel at Fjaerland. I'm so well known in these parts now that I'm accepted as a native.'

'You certainly speak the language as if you were.'

She had heard him greeting people on the quay at Balestrand, where the arrival of the cargo boat had attracted the inhabitants as if it were the main highlight of their day. It was plain that everybody knew him, and

34

that he knew everybody. He should be useful, she reflected; a mine of information. The thought brought her problem rushing back, and it was almost with a sense of shock that she realised that at last she had arrived and was within reach of her goal. A few miles further down-stream lay Vijne, no doubt as peaceful a place as this. It seemed impossible that anything so disturbing as an anonymous letter could have originated in such a serene part of the world.

As Steve steered the launch towards the landing-stage Tessa asked, 'Do you miss London? Don't you find a place like this pretty quiet by comparison?'

'I get nostalgic at times, of course, and the place doesn't swing the way London does, but I get trips back home pretty frequently and life here has more than average compensations. In fact,' he said, his eyes openly admiring, 'you can have a ball if you want to, particularly if you enjoy the great outdoors, as I do. The ski-ing, the sailing, the fishing — they're unbeatable.'

'And the climbing?'

There was the briefest hesitation. 'I don't go in for that much.'

'I'm surprised. You seem to be an all-round sportsman.'

'More or less, but climbing's too slow for me. I like speed.'

'That doesn't tie up with the temperament of a fisherman.'

He laughed, his teeth white against his tanned face, the sun lighting his blond head. 'Doesn't, does it?' he agreed. 'But fishing's a great sport.'

He tied up the launch, then helped her ashore. 'The porter will fetch your bags and put them in your cabin. Carlota — she's Thor Revold's wife and they own this place together — told me you'd applied for one in preference to a guest room in the hotel.'

'Yes — I liked the sound of them from the brochure.'

'You made a good choice. These Norwegian buildings are attractive and picturesque, but the wooden walls are thin and if it's peace and quiet you're after you won't get it in the hotel — every sound can be heard from adjoining rooms. Not,' he added, his eyes openly assessing her, 'that I'd expect anyone of your age to be seeking peace and quiet, but privacy — yes. The garden cabins certainly provide that. I have one myself — a number are reserved for staff. Each has a living-room with a sleeping alcove, plus a tiny kitchen and shower-room — like a miniature hunting lodge. If you look right of the bathing island you can see them, that group of log huts amongst the pines. Personally, I find the arrangement ideal. In my particular job it's an asset not to live in the hotel. It gets me away from the guests when off duty, which means I'm not pestered to give fishing lessons at all hours of the day and night — oh yes, we fish these waters in the dark, and night fleets go out from Balestrand regularly.'

He led her towards the hotel. Log built at the base, with weather-boarded floors above, the Nordfjord might have been a sprawling Norwegian country house, balconies and jutting eaves carved in wood, windows and walls gay with the flowering plants which were a national feature. The hotel nestled beneath fir-clad slopes on the outskirts of Fjaerland village, with a terraced garden spreading down to the narrow strip of fjord, which was quiet and smooth and vividly green. From the garden a rustic bridge led to the bathing and boating island which Hatton had indicated.

'Come and meet the Revolds,' he said now. 'You'll like Thor — he's a great guy — and you'll like Carlota too. They've gone out on a limb, building this place, and I hope it succeeds, if only to spite the pessimists who say it won't.'

37

'Why shouldn't it?'

'Because Fjaerland is off the beaten track, tucked away in this off-shoot from the main fjord, but the fishing is attracting more and more visitors, so more and more have been basing themselves at Balestrand in order to take the hour's trip here. It's been very profitable for boat-owners there, running launches to cope with the demand, not to mention full-day fishing excursions. In the last two years they've trebled the number — I ought to know; I worked at the biggest hotel there before Revold lured me away. Not that I needed much persuasion. This spot is more sheltered, which means that amateur fishermen can get more sport. Balestrand faces the widest expanse of the Sojne and sometimes only the local fishing fleets can brave the elements.'

He led her into a wide hall, panelled in Norwegian pine and colourful with flowers. A bare pine staircase swept up to a galleried first floor. 'Balustrades carved by local craftsmen,' he said. 'The furniture too.'

'It's lovely. Really lovely.'

Tessa glanced round appreciatively. The Scandinavian simplicity and character gave out a welcome which no grand hotel could equal, and she knew that in other circumstances she could be very happy here.

She felt this even more strongly later, installed in her log cabin amongst the fir trees. Steve was right — this was much better than having a room in the hotel; it was like having a small home of one's own, a snug place with a wooden floor covered with hand-woven rugs in vivid colours and intricate designs.

'You can see the weavers at work in the village,' Thor Revold had said over a welcoming drink. 'Fjaerland is famous for its crafts — weaving and carving and knitting, all in designs over a thousand years old. Boat-building too. You can still see the Viking touch in our fishing vessels.'

'I've noticed it,' Tessa had said, adding that she intended to visit the village the next day, whereupon Carlota Revold pointed out that everything was closed on Sundays. 'People are devout in these parts. Not demonstratively religious, but sincere in an unpretentious way.'

Nevertheless, someone had been devious enough to sit down and pen an anonymous note and send it hundreds of miles as a reminder of some kind. A painful reminder? What else? Now that she was alone Tessa took it out again and studied the envelope. She had done this so often, puzzling over it, becoming more and more bewildered and angry. And there was the postmark as plain as ever — *Vijne, Norge.* Only a few miles from this very spot. Now that she had arrived she found it impossible to believe that anyone would travel to so remote a region just to post a letter or to divert a scent. Anywhere along the Norwegian coast would have sufficed without undertaking a long, slow journey deep into fjord country, so surely that meant that the sender was right here, or at any rate close by?

Yet again the incessant question hammered on her brain — why should the unknown writer suddenly think of James Pickard in faraway England and take a sheet of notepaper and write a question on it? Something must have sparked the idea or brought him to mind, and since the letter was posted ten days after the Wynyard affair, the obvious supposition was that the news had been reported in the Norwegian press later, or that British newspapers had arrived belatedly in this far-distant place, the reports revealing Pickard's whereabouts to someone who remembered something from long ago and wanted to taunt him with it, to remind him and hurt him.

The more she thought about it, the more convinced Tessa became that this unexpected arrow out of the unknown had mortally wounded her father.

40

She crushed the note on a blind impulse of anger. Whoever had sent it would never get away with it. She would hunt him down and demand an explanation, hitting back in her father's defence. That was why she had come and she had to remember it. She must not be lulled by the serenity of life here, or deluded into thinking that people who lived quietly and simply were necessarily guileless.

4

There was a knock at the door. It was Steve Hatton, his handsome face smiling. 'Settled in?' he asked amiably.

'More or less. I've finished unpacking, at least.'

'How d'you like your quarters?'

'They're great. As you say, much better than being in the hotel.'

'You eat there, of course, but you'll find the portable cooker handy if you don't want to; they'll always send food down to you too — the service is good here. How about dining together tonight? It will help to break the ice for you.'

'I'd like that.'

She looked at his young, fair, likeable face, the face of a man somewhere in his late twenties — she judged him to be little older than herself, and welcomed a companion of her own age. Even so, she was suddenly comparing his frank face with the lean, dark one of the Norwegian skipper. In looks at least their nationalities should have been reversed, Tessa thought, having always believed Norwegians to be predominantly blond. The *Valkyrie*'s skipper proved otherwise; Thor Revold, too. Steve Hatton looked more of the blue-eyed young Viking than either of them and his eyes had not yet stored the deep well of experience which she had seen in the eyes of the man on the cargo ship. Steve knew his way around, but there were no dark undercurrents to his nature.

Irrelevantly, she wondered if the Norwegian was married. At his age it would be surprising if he were not, but she knew instinctively that he appreciated women, in which case marriage would make little difference to him. One moral code for his private life, another outside it. She was glad she would never meet him again.

As they walked through the garden to the hotel she said, 'I got a map of this area before I left England. There should be some good walks.'

'Plenty, if you want them. Personally, I prefer sailing. I'm no more a hiker than I am a climber.'

'That's a change. I come from an area where either is an occupational disease.'

'It's pretty much the same here, only more so. Plus ski-ing, of course. The greatest challenge in these parts is the glacier. In winter it's the greatest ski-run in the world, seventy miles long and fifty across, but it's not wise to tackle it from this direction.'

'Why not?'

'Because the point overhanging Fjaerland marks the end of it, and it's difficult to ski against the natural lie of the ice. That's the direction it has moved in summer, then settled, like a vast frozen lake of waves and crests, and the flow is always in this direction. For safety's sake you have to follow it, and in any case it's easier going because once you start ski-ing across the glacier you absolutely must keep on.'

'Does it literally overhang this place?'

'Yes — two or three miles beyond the other end of the village. Visitors cruise along this stretch of water just to gaze up at it. You can see it projecting over the mountain top like an overhanging shelf, a kind of frozen ceiling. And that's what the glacier really is, the frozen ceiling of the mountains. In summer you can hear it cracking as it moves, even from these hundreds of feet below. That's why Jostedal can only be crossed in winter, when the ice is stationary, solidified, and no crevasses are likely to split open as you approach. In summer it is constantly on the move; a mobile glacier and a danger to life.'

They climbed the steps leading into the

hotel and as he held the door open for her he continued, 'Periodically it avalanches over the side, exploding in the air like a gigantic waterfall and then thundering down. This happens only in summer and it's a sight worth seeing, especially when the sun shines on it. Incidentally, it is also the reason why the water in this small fjord is such a vivid green.'

'How's that?'

'There's a huge mass of frozen deposit at the foot of the mountain. It forms a solid tunnel. You can walk right into it if you don't mind getting wet and cold. Inside this ice tunnel there is a slow and constant thaw, but outside it's the reverse — the walls and roof are constantly being thickened by deposits from the peak. This means that a stream flows from inside the tunnel down to the fjord. It is full of minerals, minute particles which create this colour. When it reaches the Sojnc Fjord it is swallowed up, and disappears.' His attractive smile flashed. 'Knowledgeable, aren't I? To tell the truth, I learned all this from Revold.'

Tessa laughed as he held her chair and seated himself opposite, then she steered the conversation the way she wanted it to go.

'Apart from going to see the glacier, are there any other places of interest? Villages, for instance. I saw one marked on my map — Vijne. That's not far, is it?'

'A few miles, but not worth the trip. There's nothing to see there. A few scattered houses, one or two small-holdings, a cluster of village shops, a church, a post office. Nothing more than that.'

'Then why do people live there?'

'Very few do, except old people who have been there all their lives and have nowhere else to go. Others own weekend cottages at Vijne, mostly inherited and which they can't get rid of, so they come occasionally during the summer. People from as far afield as Oslo or Stavanger or Bergen. I guess they'd all be willing to sell if there was a market for such property, but no one wants a place at Vijne these days, which isn't surprising. It's just that bit too isolated to be attractive.' He thrust a menu before her and said, 'Now concentrate on that, girl. I'm hungry and you damn well ought to be after all your travelling. I can recommend the Trout Meunière — fresh from the fjord. I expect Olaf caught them this morning. You can study those pictures later.'

It wasn't until then that Tessa realised she was staring at a row of paintings on the dining-room wall. Her eyes might have been on them, but her mind was not because one thought was spinning through it. *Someone who lived in Oslo or Stavanger or Bergen* . . . not a resident at all. She acknowledged now that in coming here she might be very wide of the mark indeed.

Despair came creeping back, disappointment so bitter that she had to concentrate on the pictures to hide it. 'They're good,' she said mechanically. 'Is the artist celebrated?'

'In these parts, yes. He has a flourishing business on the side, but he's in his mid-fifties now and spends all his time painting.'

'And only the mountains. Doesn't he paint anything else?'

'Hardly ever. Mountains are his obsession. He used to be a great climber and a noted skier in his youth. Have you made up your mind yet?'

She settled for the trout and, as if mesmerised, her attention went back to the paintings. Across mountains such as these her father had ski-ed with an Allied snow corps during the war. He had been familiar with such a background before she was born. He had loved it, but had never returned. Why not? *Why not?* The unanswered question-mark loomed large in her mind again. She remembered that he had even rejected opportunities to join climbing parties there, and that when expeditions were organised for his pupils it had been Dan, not he, who accompanied them.

There must have been a reason and she puzzled over it as her gaze wandered on. The paintings were brilliant, but she scarcely saw them until she gradually became aware that they were not all of mountains. Some were of endless snow-fields, others stark seas of ice, pinnacle-spiked; glacier scenes which struck a chill into the heart but were compelling in their frozen immobility.

'He's certainly familiar with the landscape,' she said.

'So he ought to be. Lars Hyerdal is a native of these parts; born and brought up here and never lived anywhere else. I shouldn't think there's a mountain crag he doesn't know, or a single ski-run. Not to mention the villages and their inhabitants. Everyone knows Lars Hyerdal, and Lars Hyerdal knows everyone.'

Tessa felt a quickening of excitement. Here was someone else who might be useful. He might know who came and went to and from Vijne, how often, and where they lived. It would take some digging for, but she was quite prepared to dig.

'Could I visit his studio?'

'If you're interested in painting, yes. He won't welcome you otherwise.'

Then as of this moment I'm interested in painting, she decided. She had to meet this man, and soon.

5

Steve told her how to find Hyerdal's place in Balestrand.

'Take the hill behind the Kwikne Hotel and keep right on along the fjord road, past the English church of St. Olaf. A mile or so further on you'll see a large white house overlooking the fjord — you can't miss it; it stands alone. The entrance to the studio is off the side drive and the door will probably be open. Lars is a fresh-air fiend.'

★ ★ ★

Tessa sailed to Balestrand two days later, praying that the visit would prove more rewarding than the one she had paid to Vijne the day after her arrival. The place had fulfilled Steve's description down to the last detail — a cluster of lonely houses, village shops, a church, no more. She had walked the length of the village without seeing a single friendly face, and was not surprised. After a dismal prowl about the place she had caught the bus back to Fjaerland gladly. An empty bus. That hadn't surprised her either.

But Balestrand was a different proposition; small, but alive, with a busy ferry and an industrious atmosphere. No air of desolation here; a lively and attractive place hugging the shores of the mighty fjord. She followed Steve's instructions and found Hyerdal's house with ease.

Walking down the side drive she saw the studio door, and Steve was right again — it was open. When she stepped inside she was astonished by the size and space, a vast room with immense windows on three sides, admitting both the maximum of light and view. The wide sweep of the Sojne seemed to surround the house and she realised that it stood on a projection, with a steeply sloping garden. This was certainly an artist's paradise, particularly for one who loved mountains. They formed a permanent backcloth to the scene from all sides, towering peaks jutting into the heavens or sweeping in vast ranges of overlapping folds.

'You seem more interested in my view than in my paintings,' a tired voice said.

She spun round. A man in a wheelchair was framed in an open doorway.

'I'm sorry — I thought the room was empty. I didn't hear you come in.'

'Of course you didn't.' A long hand

gestured towards the rubber tyres of the chair. 'You don't think I want to trundle round my house rattling like some ancient steam engine, do you?'

Tessa laughed, and a corner of his bearded chin tilted, his mouth curving in unwilling response. Steve had said that this man was in his mid-fifties. He looked more. Worse than that, she felt he had lost the ability to be amused and didn't want to regain it. Up to a point she could sympathise, for she herself was only just learning how to laugh again, emerging from the shock of her father's death very slowly. It was Steve who was helping her to do that, and to feel young again, and for this Tessa was grateful. Time and youth were on her side, but this man in the wheelchair lacked both. She felt a swift pity for him.

'Well,' Hyerdal said gruffly, 'how do you like them? My pictures, I mean.'

'I'm no judge. I know little about art.'

'You don't need knowledge or lessons in art appreciation to know whether you like a picture or not. Do you like mine?'

Despite his words, his tone implied that if she didn't she was no judge. Tessa had heard of the artistic ego, but didn't feel inclined to pander to it despite pity for the man. If it came to that, she wasn't sure that he needed her pity. He was successful and, she suspected, self-centred.

'I like some,' she answered candidly. 'Not all.'

'That's honest, at least. What brought you here?'

She couldn't reveal that. She couldn't tell him that she had come in the hope of getting information out of him, some clue about a person or persons, inadvertently dropped in the course of conversation. She didn't say she had hoped he would be easy to talk to, a garrulous sort of man who would let slip precious titbits about local inhabitants or visitors because Steve had said that everyone knew him and he knew everyone. That might well be, but she judged Lars Hyerdal to be introverted and withdrawn, and with acute disappointment realised that the long shot she had taken in coming here was going to prove a wasted effort after all. All she could do was display a polite interest in his work, and then go, so she strolled about the studio, studying the paintings and leaving him to his easel. He had picked up his brushes and was cleaning them with a smelly turpentine rag, clearly forgetting her. If she slipped away, he wouldn't even notice her departure.

She was about to leave when a voice said, 'I've brought some coffee, Father.'

Once more Tessa spun round. She knew that voice. It belonged to *Valkyrie*'s skipper and there he was now, staring at her with ironical recognition.

The nautical sweater had gone; in its place he wore a white turtle-necked shirt with well-tailored slacks and casual shoes. In a remote corner of her mind she thought how deeply tanned his face looked against the white shirt and how surprising it was that he fitted so well into this background of comfort. She hadn't imagined him in a house like this. She hadn't associated him with anything but a rolling deck or lofty peaks.

His father said drily, 'I see you two have met before.'

'On *Valkyrie*,' his son told him, setting down the coffee tray. 'Her name is Tessa. Suits her, don't you think? I'll fetch another cup.'

When they were alone again, Hyerdal's glance raked her.

'Now I know why you came, young lady. Not to see my work, but to see Max. A shallow pretence, if I may say so.' She was about to make a frosty retort when he added, 'Don't bother to deny it. I can tell when a man and a woman are aware of each other.'

Tessa felt an urgent desire to get away

from here. She didn't like this man or his son, but a moment later Max Hyerdal reappeared, forestalling departure. His glance was again ironical as he poured coffee and handed her a cup, and she knew he was not only amused but fully aware that she had come by chance and was regretting it.

'So you were a passenger on one of our ships, were you?' his father said. 'I hope you were comfortable.'

'Thank you. I was.'

'My son is a good skipper. Capable at his job. But it isn't his greatest interest in life. Nor was it mine. My grandfather started the business with one cargo vessel and now it is the busiest line on the whole of our western coast. Naturally we are proud of that, but such success cannot compare with conquering nature. My dear young lady, you are not drinking your coffee.'

'It's hot,' she said, but took a gulp, determined to get it down and then leave. All the time she could feel Max Hyerdal's penetrating glance and to cover confusion she said at random, 'By conquering nature I presume you mean conquering those mountains. Climbing, in fact.'

'Yes. The triumph of man over peak and glacier. The challenge is greater than peddling cargo. The war gave me the chance to get out of that. My brother was alive then and ran the line until he died two years ago.'

'And after the war?'

'That is self-evident, surely?' The man nodded towards a distant cabinet. 'See that photograph over there? I keep it as a reminder. Take a look at it.'

'Father . . . ' There was a note of protest in his son's voice.

'Don't be absurd, Max. Why shouldn't the girl see it? It can mean nothing to her.'

Tessa looked at Hyerdal's son and saw concern in his eyes, almost a warning, but she walked across the studio and picked up the photograph. It was of a strong, upright man somewhere in his late twenties; a vigorous man in the climbing uniform of a mountain regiment, with a load of equipment on his back.

Her breath caught.

'Is this . . . ?'

Max nodded. 'Yes. My father before the glacier did this to him.'

Lars Hyerdal's voice rasped bitterly, 'It wasn't the glacier that ruined my life, and you know it.'

6

She didn't know how she finally escaped from Lars Hyerdal's studio, but was vaguely aware that Max helped her, turning the conversation away from one which might have been difficult and embarrassing to something more trite and conventional — the influx of tourists and the increasing popularity of Norway as a winter sports ground. Something like that. Tessa scarcely paid attention, substituting polite noises as acknowledgements rather than answering any remarks specifically. She felt uncomfortable, not merely because she had come face to face with *Valkyrie*'s skipper again, but because she had walked into an atmosphere of tension which emanated from the embittered man in the wheelchair. She wondered how he managed to paint as well as he did in such circumstances.

Max walked back with her along the fjord road. She had known instinctively that he would, and he knew instinctively that she didn't want him to. That, of course, was why he did so. She accepted the gesture with apparent indifference, refusing to give him the satisfaction of showing displeasure.

She knew what would happen if she did. His eyes would mock her again, so she gave him no chance. At the end of the fjord road was the ferry. She would be rid of him there.

But when the house was left behind he said, 'Don't be distressed by my father. His moods aren't always black and bitter.'

'I hope not, or he would be a bad psychological case.'

She didn't ask what prompted Hyerdal's outburst. She didn't want to know. Millions of people in the world had been embittered by ill-health and suffering, but others had risen above it; others far less fortunate than the middle-aged and obviously well-to-do Norwegian.

'I suppose, in a way, he is a psychological case,' Max said, half to himself.

'Aren't we all?' She kept her tone light, not wanting to be drawn into the dark circle of Lars Hyerdal's mind. 'What surprises me is that he can paint with such life and vitality when it's obvious that he no longer enjoys living. Ice and snow are cold subjects for a painter, but he gives them life if not warmth.'

'That's due to his love of the scene.'

'And he still loves it, despite what the glacier did to him?'

'Yes, despite what the glacier did to him.'

Tessa realised that Max Hyerdal had no intention of telling her the story of his father's accident, and wondered whether her reluctance to hear it had been evident. At once she was repentant, aware that she shouldn't allow herself to be submerged in her own problems to the exclusion of others, so she said impulsively, 'If you want to tell me about it, go ahead.'

'I don't. The incident is personal and private.'

'*Touché.*'

'I didn't mean it that way. I mean that I see no reason for inflicting it on strangers.'

'I've always understood that it's easier to confide in strangers than in relatives or friends — I suppose because you know you'll never meet up with strangers again and therefore you escape the embarrassment of coming face to face with them, aware that you've betrayed a confidence you would have preferred to keep to yourself.'

'But this isn't a confidence of that kind. The cause of my father's accident is well known in these parts. Stick around long enough and you're sure to hear it. I don't want to tell you right now because I want to spend the time getting acquainted. God knows, I tried hard enough on *Valkyrie*, but I'm a sticker so I'll keep right on. Where did you disappear to when you left the ship? I looked around for you, but you'd gone.'

'I thought we had said goodbye. Your exit line at the end of our conversation implied it.'

'What did you expect from a man you were determined to get rid of?'

'Not persistence, at least.'

'So I'm grateful to fate for giving me a hand.'

'Do you believe in fate?'

'Let's say it can play some very odd tricks at times. Obliging ones too, like bringing you bang into my home.'

'That's not so very odd. I gather your father's studio attracts many visitors.'

'Not always so welcome.'

'I didn't feel particularly so.'

'I'm sorry if that's true, but you didn't catch my father at his best.'

'It was something more than that. He just didn't like me. I could feel it. Perhaps he shares your aversion for the British. If so, I'll keep away, not to please either him or you, but because I've no time for prejudices, either personal or racial.'

'You don't expect me to believe that you've never disliked someone strongly? What else would you call your first reaction to me?'

'*Touché* again,' she said, and laughed.

He smiled and held out his hand. To have refused to take it would have been churlish. Besides, to her surprise she didn't want to. She stood for a moment with her hand in his, looking up at him. His face was as strong and craggy as the landscape, and if the simile wasn't flattering it was somehow apt. He seemed to reflect the ruggedness of his country. Its handsomeness too.

Behind him the ground rose in mountainous tiers on which carved Norwegian houses were perched as if some giant hand had casually dropped them. At any moment she expected a man with an umbrella or a lady with a parasol to pop out on a spring, forecasting the weather. She had had one of those little carved houses as a child, but where it had come from or who had given it to her she couldn't recall. Perhaps her father had brought it back amongst his kit after the war, but if so it couldn't have been for her. He was unmarried then, although he had wasted no time in remedying that, meeting and marrying Ruth with a haste which seemed very much out of character with the quiet, deliberate man his daughter had known. It was this lack of haste in his make-up which had made him the great climber he was. A mountain was no place for the impatient, he always said, and anyone who tackled it hurriedly was sure to fail.

Even his face had shown resolution, combined with that deep repose which characterises men who spend their lives battling with the elements or overcoming obstacles. Max Hyerdal had it too. Tessa was struck by the similarity between the two men, not in feature or figure or personality, for James Pickard had been thick-set and square-featured and quiet, whereas Max was tall and lithe and decidedly extrovert, but they shared a quality of strength found only in men who met hazards calmly.

Her glance wandered to the rocky ledges above, with their toy houses and tiny terraced plots. Every bit of level ground was tilled and planted, and she was fascinated by clothes-lines of waving grass hanging out to dry. 'I've never seen that before,' she said.

His glance followed.

'Grass is a precious commodity here. We have no farms like you have in England, not in this mountainous terrain at least, so every scrap of earth has to be made good use of, and every blade of grass saved for winter fodder. Have you seen this little church?' He opened a gate beside him. 'If so, you'll know it is for the English community here. It's interesting — let me show you.'

St. Olaf's was a quaint wooden construction,

with carved scrolls and gargoyles adorning the exterior, the interior, also of unstained wood, featuring a colourful selection of hand-painted ecclesiastical pictures. 'All done by local artists,' Max said.

She studied the signatures and saw that none belonged to his father. Somehow this wasn't surprising.

As they walked downhill towards the ferry Max said, 'If you're a churchgoer I expect you'll be attending there?'

Tessa laughed. 'Why don't you ask outright if I am staying in Balestrand? It's what you're trying to find out, isn't it?'

'Okay — so I'll ask outright. *Are* you staying in Balestrand, and if so, where?'

'No — I'm not.' She threw the answer over her shoulder as she ran down to the quayside where Olaf was loading the Revolds' supply launch with provisions. 'Nordfjord Hotel' was painted clearly on bow and stern, so Max Hyerdal could see for himself where she was bound for. Olaf was lifting the final lot aboard, so she hauled in the fenders and he cast off. 'Goodbye,' she called to Max, 'and thanks for the coffee.'

'You're wrong,' he called back. 'It's not goodbye. I have craft of my own.'

It was ridiculous to feel pleased. She really had nothing to be pleased about, for the day had been a failure, yielding no helpful information and bringing her no nearer to her goal.

★ ★ ★

A few days later the first stroke of luck came her way. One of the receptionists — the only one who spoke fluent English — was called to nurse her sick mother in Oslo, and departed at once. It was an opportunity too good to miss; Tessa promptly volunteered to help, feeling ashamed when Carlota and Thor thanked her profusely and insisted upon remunerating her, including her cabin accommodation as part of it. 'All employees are entitled to accommodation,' Carlota insisted, 'and so long as you fill the gap, you're an employee and a welcome one. It is *you* who are doing *us* a favour, believe me — with so many American and English visitors now coming, an English receptionist is heaven-sent.'

Tessa accepted with good grace, hiding the fact that her motive was to meet people, particularly local residents. As a holidaymaker she couldn't hope to get 'on the inside', and it was only by being accepted in this way that she was likely to learn anything about the inhabitants, or pick up a thread which might lead her to Vijne and the writer of the anonymous letter.

She took up her duties at once. The work was straight-forward and she mastered it quickly. Her time was regulated, giving her ample opportunity to meet people both in the course of work and outside it. It was Steve, not she, who was pestered by holidaymakers; he was perpetually in demand for either fishing or sailing lessons, whereas all she had to do was desk work, then relax when off duty. On top of this the atmosphere was congenial, thanks to the Revolds, who made her feel very much at home. Although they never intruded upon her free time, they made it plain that she was welcome to spend it with them whenever she felt so inclined. They introduced her to their friends and included her in outings, so she wasn't surprised a week or two after her encounter with the Hyerdals when Carlota invited her on a trip to Voss, timing it to fit in with Tessa's off-duty period.

It was a long, slow journey, but she was becoming accustomed to long, slow journeys in a part of the world where much of it was done by fjord steamer, but this time Olaf took them in the hotel's fastest launch direct to Flaam, thereby saving innumerable stops at fjord villages and enabling them to catch the small electric railway which zigzagged up two thousand feet of mountainside, across clefts and gorges and beneath cascading waterfalls, to lofty Myrdal. There they boarded the main Oslo — Bergen train, arriving at Voss in the afternoon.

Standing beside its huge lake, the small town was humming with visitors, some *en route* to the high ski-slopes which offered sport to the enthusiasts even in summer. This combination of summer sun and winter snow was new and exciting to Tessa, and for the first time since her arrival in Norway her mind rejected all thought of the anonymous note. The air at this height was like wine and as they walked along the lakeside to their hotel she was conscious of a feeling of exhilaration. This spell-binding country never ran out of spectacular views, and she was delighted to find that her hotel room looked right across the water towards the historic stave church for which Voss was famous.

But Carlota had her mind on more practical things, the first being hairdressing appointments. Voss had a beauty parlour which offered the whole works — sauna baths, slimming treatments, facials — 'Plus one of the best hairdressers for miles around,' Carlota said. 'Kerstin is sure to fit us in, if only to please her mother.'

'Who is her mother?'

'Margrit Amundsen. You must have seen her — she dined with us last weekend. She works in Balestrand and often visits us on her free day, which is usually Saturday or Sunday because on those days the cargo vessels don't run.'

'You mean the Hyerdal Line?'

'Yes. She virtually runs the office since Max has to supervise the voyages. Poor Margrit — she lost her husband when Kerstin was only ten, and was left very badly off. The job at Hyerdal's was heaven-sent, but sometimes I think she demonstrates her gratitude a little too much.'

'In what way?'

'She's too conscientious by far. I'm always urging her to ease up, but the poor soul is so terrified of losing her job that she takes on more than she should.'

'And Max lets her? What sort of man is that?'

Their rooms were linked with an intervening bathroom and conversation took place as they unpacked, communicating doors open. Now Carlota crossed the bathroom and stood leaning against the door frame, looking at Tessa with a direct and candid glance which was characteristic of her.

'I'll tell you what sort of a man he is — the sort any woman would jump at.'

'Then why hasn't somebody jumped? I gather he's still unmarried.'

Carlota laughed. 'Yes — in his thirties and very eligible. I guess he has always jumped out of the way. Not because he doesn't like women, but possibly because he likes them a little too much.'

'Meaning that he takes his pleasure where he can find it, but dodges responsibility?'

Carlota shrugged.

'What man doesn't, if he can get away with it? Not that he'll do so for much longer if Margrit's ambitions are fulfilled.'

'But she must be twenty years older!'

Carlota laughed. 'Her ambitions aren't for herself — they're for Kerstin. Her daughter and Max would make an ideal couple. Everyone expects them to marry and I wouldn't be surprised if they did. They're almost inseparable when she comes home, and he visits her in Voss very often. I suspect they meet elsewhere in between.'

Tessa's stab of disappointment was swift and unreasonable. To cover it she said, 'Kerstin will get a difficult father-in-law if she does marry Max.'

'Poor Lars. Life has been cruel to him.'

'I know.' She thought of her own father's

tragic death, and of the injustice preceding it. 'Life is cruel to many people, in many different ways.'

'That's true, but Lars has had more than his share, and when Nina left him that was the deepest cut of all.'

'Nina?'

'His wife.'

Tessa was surprised, having taken it for granted that Lars Hyerdal was a widower.

'What was she like?' she asked curiously. 'And why did she leave him?'

'Why does any woman desert a man? Because she no longer loves him, or because she loves someone else, or because she is bored and wants a life more interesting than he can give her — and sometimes because he is a burden.'

'Surely you don't mean that Nina Hyerdal walked out on her husband because he was a cripple?'

'It's the general belief. There seemed no other reason. Margrit is the only one who defends her. To be more accurate I should say that Margrit is the only one who doesn't condemn her. We can't judge other people's lives or actions, she always says.'

'She's right. I like the sound of Margrit.'

'Well, I'm afraid I'm not the saint she is. I do condemn Nina Hyerdal for

69

deserting a man who not only loved her but needed her. Love shouldn't place an obligation on others, that's merely being possessive, but need most definitely does. We can't go through life deserting people who are physically handicapped and therefore dependent upon us.'

Tessa remembered Lars Hyerdal's bitter outburst. '*It wasn't the glacier that ruined my life.*' Now she knew what he meant, and pity stirred.

'What was his wife like?'

'Very lovely. That was why she was able to take off for a new life in Oslo, even in middle age. A plainer woman would have stayed at home, afraid to take such a chance at her time of life.'

'Then she didn't desert her son when he was a child?'

'No, the break-up came when Max had grown up. I suppose a boy about the house kept it lively and full of young people, and Nina loved life. I didn't know her as well as Margrit did, they were at school together, but I do remember that at every party and every dance men gravitated towards Nina. I think the fact that she was English added to her attraction; made her just that little bit different from the rest of us.'

'Had Nina grown up in Norway?'

'She was born here. Her father was English and came to the British Consulate in Oslo as a young man, with his English bride.'

Tessa remembered Max's references to his English grandparents, but still couldn't understand that strong impression she had received of an aversion for the British. 'One in particular,' he had said, and she had assumed he meant herself. Now she wondered. He could have meant his English mother, who had deserted his crippled father. 'Stick around long enough and you're sure to hear the story,' he had said the other day, and now she had heard part of it.

But curiosity about Nina Hyerdal wasn't so great as curiosity about Kerstin Amundsen, which was soon, and devastatingly, satisfied; devastatingly because she turned out to be one of the prettiest girls Tessa had seen for a long time. The tall, blonde Scandinavian type. In the beauty parlour mirror her reflection more than eclipsed Tessa's own, even when her skilled fingers had made the utmost of Tessa's very ordinary brown hair.

'I didn't know the Revolds had a new receptionist,' Kerstin said as she put the finishing touches. 'My mother didn't tell me.'

'She probably doesn't know. We haven't met. I saw her dining with Carlota and Thor last weekend, but she probably didn't notice me. Do you come to the Sojne often, or do you spend your weekends here?'

'That depends.'

'On what? Or should I say on whom?'

Kerstin smiled, an attractive mouth curving on beautiful teeth.

'On whom, yes.'

She gave a final spray to Tessa's hair and held up a mirror so that she could view the back. 'Of course,' she continued, 'I pay duty visits to Balestrand to see my mother. Not that she expects me to — not regularly, anyway. She knows that Max has first call on me. If he is berthed at Bergen or Stavanger at weekends, I join him there, but if he's home I go to Balestrand and stay with my mother — then Max and I get in some climbing. Mother is very understanding.'

'So it seems.'

'I expect you've heard of Max Hyerdal,' Kerstin added, taking a pad out of her pocket and writing out the bill.

'More than that — I've met him.'

The paper made a sharp little sound as Kerstin tore it from the pad.

'In that case you'll be interested to hear what a keen climber he is. Most of us are in this part of the world.'

'I know. We do it at home too.'

'In *England*?'

'Yes. The Lake District. Also Snowdonia in Wales and the Highlands of Scotland. The mountains aren't so immense as the Alps, of course, but they give good climbing. Treacherous, too, in places like Glencoe.'

'You should take the chance to learn while you are here.'

'I may do that,' Tessa answered easily. 'Max has offered to teach me.'

But there was no ruffling Kerstin Amundsen's cool composure. If anything, her smile was even more serene.

'That's characteristic of him. He's always willing to help beginners. I shouldn't pass up the opportunity, if I were you.'

Just for that, Tessa thought, I damn well won't, and I don't mind if you're around to watch the first lesson, Miss Amundsen.

Aloud, she said negligently, 'I'll think about it. It may help to pass the time. And thank you for doing my hair so beautifully.'

This last she meant sincerely, and they parted with the usual show of affability displayed by two people who don't care if they never meet again.

7

Two things happened the following weekend. On Saturday evening Tessa met Margrit Amundsen for the first time, and on Sunday she went climbing with Max. The first event wasn't momentous, but the second was.

She was on duty at the reception desk when Margrit's tall erect figure climbed the steps of the hotel and pushed open the swing doors. Tessa looked up automatically and at that precise moment the woman looked at her. Kerstin's mother was handsome but unspectacular, and Tessa's immediate impression was of someone a little unsure of herself. Shy, perhaps, or merely reserved. She said good evening and the woman smiled pleasantly but a little hesitantly.

'Are you wanting to see Mrs. Revold?' Tessa asked. 'She's in her flat. I can ring through and let her know you're here.'

The Revolds lived on the premises, in a flat at the rear of the hotel.

'Thank you, but she's expecting me. I rang her earlier and told her I'd be passing this way.'

Passing? To where could one pass from

Fjaerland village except to other villages even more remote, and why should anyone want to? Tessa didn't know why the question flashed through her mind, except that visitors to the Nordfjord Hotel either came to stay, or to lunch or dine. They certainly never went any further, except to sail on to the far outskirts of Fjaerland to see the over-hanging glacier then returning to the hotel, which was a convenient place at which to terminate a fjord trip, or to visit specifically for its good food.

'Then I don't need to announce you — go right ahead.' Tessa accompanied the remark with a smile.

But Margrit Amundsen didn't go right ahead. She stood for a moment looking at the girl, then walked slowly towards the desk — a neat, well-turned-out woman in neat, well-turned-out clothes, tweeds and sensible walking shoes chosen with a reasonable eye for style. Her appearance couldn't really be faulted, from the crown of her smooth head, blonde hair turning to grey, to her long slim legs. But, even so, in some subtle way she missed being striking. Kerstin resembled her closely, but Tessa doubted if this woman had ever been as lovely as her daughter, although basically, in figure and feature, they were similar.

'You must be the new receptionist from England. Carlota told me about you. I hope you are enjoying life here?'

'I am — very much. You're Mrs. Amundsen, aren't you? I met your daughter the other day. She's very lovely.'

Margrit Amundsen's eyes lit up. 'She is, isn't she?' It was obvious that Kerstin was her mother's pride and joy. 'She's here this weekend. In Balestrand, I mean.'

That meant to see Max. The girl had described her visits to her mother as no more than duty ones, admitting that Max had first call on her. Tessa wondered if Margrit knew this and if she minded. If Carlota's verdict was correct and this woman was intent upon marriage between the two then, far from minding, she should be pleased.

Mrs. Amundsen gave a brief little smile accompanied by what Tessa felt to be an oddly searching glance, a glance of question and curiosity which was hard to understand. If she was sizing her up as a possible rival for her daughter where Max was concerned, she had nothing to worry about. Tessa gave a mental shrug as the woman disappeared towards the Revolds' quarters, then got on with her work. Half an hour later she went off duty and as she walked through the grounds towards her cabin she saw Steve sailing towards the boating island with a passenger aboard, an hotel guest returning from a sailing lesson. Steve hailed her.

'What are you doing tonight?' he called through cupped hands.

'Grilling a chop, doing my nails, and going to bed with a book,' she called back.

'What a waste!'

The passenger laughed, a middle-aged American who obviously sensed a romance between them. Tessa went on her way with a casual wave of the hand. She liked Steve, but something made her resist the idea of being paired off with him in anyone's mind, especially his own. She had had enough indications from him that he wouldn't be averse to the idea. That was sufficient to put up her resistance. Apart from Dan waiting for her back home — with increasing impatience from the sound of his letters — she liked her job here, was more relaxed, happier than when she first came, but for the remainder of her stay she wanted no complications, no involvements. At any rate, not with Steve.

She dodged the implication of that and gave herself up to pleasurable anticipation of a leisurely evening. She didn't feel in the mood for dining in the hotel and possibly having to make polite conversation with people. She was in the mood for solitude and an early night, so when the 'phone rang a few minutes later she swore. Steve was being persistent.

'I've told you my plans for the evening,' she said without any preliminaries, 'and I'm not changing my mind.'

'You haven't told *me*,' said Max, 'and it isn't this evening I'm calling about, but tomorrow. Will you be free?'

'Why — yes — yes, I'll be free.' Surprise made her stammer.

'Then how about a climbing lesson?'

'I'd like that, but what about Kerstin?'

'She'll come too,' he answered easily. 'Can you be ready by eleven?'

'Of course.'

'We won't try anything strenuous to start. A little hill-climbing, that's all, so you'll only need a stout pair of climbing boots, which you can get at the hotel. They keep a good stock, I know. Some tough trousers and a sweater and you'll be all set. Carlota will lend you an anorak, although if this weather holds you won't need it. I'll bring anything else that's necessary.'

'Fine,' she said, smiling to herself. She had no need to ask the Revolds to open up the hotel shop after hours; she had all the necessary climbing gear, obeying Dan's injunction to pack her kit. What she didn't

78

like was the idea of being third in a party of two, especially when the two were Max and Kerstin, so after a bit of thought she rang Steve and invited him along.

'Well, I'm not very partial to climbing, but I am to you, chick, so I'll join up.'

'Thanks, Steve. Thanks a lot.'

'But if you're thinking of pairing me off with Kerstin, don't try. I like her, but I like you better. Apart from that, she's labelled Max's property and I'm not trespassing.'

'There'll be no pairing off as far as I'm concerned. The four of us together.'

'That's a pity,' he said cheerfully, 'but if that's the way you want it . . . '

That was the way she did want it, and the way she intended it to be.

Before going to bed Tessa checked her gear and packed her rucksack in readiness. That would be surprise number one, she thought, and was right. Although he made no comment when they met next morning, she saw Max's eyes take in every detail of her outfit, from the light-weight anorak to the commando-soled boots. She had given careful thought to footwear, deciding on Vibram soles rather than spikes because Max intended this to be a beginner's lesson, which meant tackling slopes where spikes weren't likely to be needed. All the same, she had put a pair of crampons in her rucksack, just in case.

Almost on the dot his launch drew alongside the hotel's jetty. The morning was fine and sunny, lighting up Kerstin's fair hair. Her climbing outfit was elegant as well as practical, or her lovely figure made it appear so, and although Tessa was prepared to be eclipsed by her she felt a momentary pang of envy. Her own stout jeans and much-worn anorak weren't designed to enhance the appearance. She had worn them for years, and was suddenly aware that this was only too evident.

They walked to the near outskirts of the village because the overhanging glacier shelf at the far end ruled out climbing in that vicinity and, on reaching the foothills which skirted the higher mountain slopes, began a gentle hill-climb through scrub and scree. Max led, followed by Kerstin, with Steve and Tessa bringing up the rear. This was the kind of hill walk which James would have described as 'one which you could take with your hands in your pockets', a sentence which conveys so much to a mountaineer that it might well be used to distinguish fell-walking from rock-climbing. She looked up and with an unexpected little pang of pleasure saw out-thrusts of rock high above.

She hoped they would get that far because, pleasant as hill-walking could be, rock-faces presented greater interest and challenge.

For the first time since her father's death Tessa felt a quickening of delight, the thrill of expectation which even an average climber feels at the start of an expedition. She hadn't imagined that she could feel like this ever again, but suddenly she was remembering a day when she and James had climbed Great Gable at home. High up, it was a cool autumn day, and below were clouds, surging up from the Irish Sea and over Wast-water, then following the upsweep of Styhead Pass and down the other side towards Stockley Bridge.

They had capped the day by abseiling three hundred feet down to the foot of the highest crag, then climbing the rock-face to Gable summit again, and there they were once more — above the clouds in the sun, on firm rough rock, filled with a sense of satisfaction and achievement and shared enjoyment, then James had put his hand on her shoulder and said, 'Well done, Tessa,' and it had been worth all the effort plus the moment of apprehension she had felt as she swung out down the rope, even though she knew that in her father's hands it was safer than any mountain rope could be. Even on a short drop she never failed to experience that apprehensive first twinge, but always hid it determinedly and afterwards forgot it in the exhilaration of the climb.

That feeling of exhilaration came to her now and she slipped automatically into the relaxed, slow, steady rhythm which she had been taught and which, ahead, Max and Kerstin were also using. Beside her, Steve climbed less easily. He was putting too much effort into it, and although he obviously knew something about the rudiments of the game he had either been badly taught or just hadn't the makings of a climber. Or maybe he had given up too soon because the sport didn't come so easily to him as other sports did. Tessa wondered if he was the kind who would abandon something unless he could master it quickly, the kind who wanted to excel, so unless he could shine he would very soon bow out. He had been wise to stick to sailing and the other activities which he was so well qualified to teach.

They had been climbing at a steady pace for about an hour when Max halted and looked back.

'Tired?' he called. 'Like a rest?'

Tessa wasn't in the least tired, and said so. He looked at her quizzically, a little smile curving his hard mouth. Hard? That was how she had first seen it, but now the word resolute seemed more apt. Resolute, with a touch of wry humour. 'Good,' he said. 'Then we'll go higher.'

By lunch-time the crags were well within sight. 'You've done well,' Max said briefly, as they sat down and opened their rucksacks. She caught his sideways glance and wondered if he observed the contents of her own. If so, it was a certain give-away, for no amateur would have packed the light-weight windproof over-trousers and other gear which were part of the professional's equipment in case weather conditions forced one to spend a night in the open. This mountain slope would afford plenty of bivouacs in that event, but in this mild summer weather it wasn't likely to occur.

She closed the flap of her rucksack casually and munched the chocolate and raisins she had brought. One glimpse of her food supply would also betray her, for she knew what to bring in the way of vitamin nourishment. How to carry it, too, in a sealed polythene bag. She regretted being so proficient, having come with the intention of surprising this man, but it wasn't time to surprise him yet.

However, he made no comment except to ask, after they had eaten and rested, whether they felt like going further.

'Of course!' Kerstin cried. 'We haven't even started yet.' She smiled vividly. She was enjoying herself, stimulated by the fresh air and the scenery and the physical exercise. So was Tessa, and when Max turned to her and said, 'How about you?' she replied that she was ready whenever he was.

'For a beginner, you're doing well,' he remarked.

'Are you surprised?' Steve put in. 'She comes from the Peak District. Anyone who knows anything about England knows that is hill country.'

'But not everyone who lives there goes hill-climbing,' she said off-handedly, and went ahead without waiting. It was only a matter of minutes before Max pulled abreast and from then on they climbed side by side, Kerstin following with Steve, positions subtly reversed. But not for long. Max's expertise was way ahead and he took the lead inevitably, heading towards the crags which now began to appear like a bas-relief against the sky. She could see overhangs which no amateur could tackle and wasn't surprised when Max veered in the direction of a conveniently grooved buttress which would make easy climbing, the sort of area on which it was ideal to learn.

But although, on approach, distant rock-faces can seem to be startlingly near, Tessa knew that at least an hour's good going would be necessary before they reached this goal, and wondered what would happen then. Would Max call a halt, then lead the descent, or would he offer the challenge she hoped for?

The challenge came. At length, he paused below a projection consisting of two sheer rock-faces — nothing to an experienced climber, but a tough initiation for a beginner. This didn't intimidate her because she had scaled crags far steeper, but his pause was an obvious question. Did she want to go ahead or turn back?

'This is where your climbing lesson really begins,' he said, 'because cliffs like this can only be tackled one way, whether they be fifty feet or one thousand feet high. Mountaineers must tackle them in pairs, on the same rope, one at a time. Do you feel like trying? If so, we'll take it together.'

'I came for a lesson, didn't I?'

She could feel Kerstin watching and knew she was expected to quail. Instead, she glanced upwards, estimating the height of the first step to be only about thirty feet, requiring a very simple climbing sequence.

The one beyond was much steeper and more precipitous.

'O.K.,' said Max, 'then here goes.'

He scaled the first face in one 'run out', belayed the rope at the top, then called to Kerstin to tie the other end of the rope to Tessa. She submitted meekly while the Norwegian girl did a job which she could have done equally well herself.

'Now!'

Max's voice called from above, and Tessa began to climb. She expected him to issue commands about footholds and how to take them, but he didn't. She could feel his eyes watching from above and the strong hold of the rope as he played it out to her.

Every cliff-face varies and on this variation depends a climber's approach. Even the friendliest crag looks smooth and therefore unscalable from a distance, but examination at close quarters reveals that the rock is broken up by cracks of all sizes, ledges of all proportions, and wrinkled faces at all angles. She sized them up and decided on her method of approach, at once forgetful of everything and everyone but the job in hand. The half-way ledge between the lower face and the upper one gave a useful two-pitch climb, and at length she landed beside Max.

He looked down at her, still with that quizzical smile. 'Well done. Ready to try the next part?'

'I'm ready to try anything within reason,' she answered meekly.

'Right.'

Without more ado, he embarked on the upper face, Tessa following as and when he commanded. It was a fairly tough climb but not too arduous, and they accomplished it in the length of time it would have taken James Pickard and his daughter to do it together.

As Max coiled the rope round his body again he uttered no word of congratulation, but cupped his hands about his mouth and yelled down to the others, 'We'll proceed to the easy slope westwards and make the descent there on foot. Care to meet us at the base, or are you coming up?'

Steve shouted back, 'We'll meet you there.' His voice echoed in the clear mountain air and, peering down, Tessa saw him start on the grassy stretch which curved at the foot of the buttress, with Kerstin following reluctantly. Either he didn't relish the climb, or didn't want to be leader on the second rope.

She followed Max along a wide ledge running below the upper stretches of a peak which pointed like a giant finger into the sky above. He obviously had no intention of taking her up there — time alone was against that idea, and to do so would have been plainly calling her bluff. So she knew he had something else in mind. He was obviously familiar with this section of the buttress and as the route was wide and made the going easy they were able to walk side by side, relaxing into the rhythmic walk which enables climbers to untense their muscles, relish the sweet air, and enjoy the scenic panorama which unfolds the higher they climb. On their left, the valley side, she saw the vast reaches of the Sojne beyond the narrower ribbon of the Fjaerland Fjord, but the village itself was cut from view. They passed a bulging slope which presented a fairly easy descent, but Max ignored it and went on, until suddenly sheer rock jutted out from the mountainside, the forerunner of a great wall of grooves and gullies and sheer slab-faces. Now what was he going to test her with? Not a slab-face, she hoped, with its undercut and pressure handholds, never a favourite of hers.

She needn't have worried. The test proved to be a hidden chimney, sharp, short, and vertical, piercing the rock above. She felt a swift relief, knowing that she could cope with this, for the lakelands offered plenty of experience in this line. Besides, she had always found chimneys an exciting part of climbing, breaching overhangs and holdless wall-faces, but giving a sense of security by virtue of their containing walls, the way to tackle them being like chimney-sweeps of old, when chimneys were wide enough to scale by backing up or straddling.

'Now watch me and do what I do,' Max ordered.

He dealt with the rope then began the ascent. Before it was her turn to follow she clipped crampons on to the soles of her boots, then began to climb. By bracing both legs with her back against the wall she could stay supported in comfort and this she did each time Max's rope signalled for her to move to his timing. Looking up, she could see his strong body wedged between the chimney walls like a human chockstone, then moving upwards again as he brought one leg below his body and then behind him, pressing his boot on the rear wall and down-wards with his hands at about waist-level, then levering his back into the higher contact with the rear wall again. Then another pause, with both boots returning against the far wall in the initial chockstone or resting position. In this way, unhurriedly, they climbed in unison until, near the top, she waited while Max hauled himself over the edge then pulled her up on the rope.

They stood looking at each other, exhilarated, triumphant, smiling. He put his arms around her and hugged her. 'You fraud,' he said. 'You've been stringing me along. How shall I punish you?'

She gave a breathless little laugh and his mouth came down to hers. They kissed happily, then at length and with passion. She felt as if the whole world had reawakened for her.

After a time she said without enthusiasm, 'We ought to join the others.'

'Not yet . . . not yet . . . '

At this point there was a smooth mossy bed upon the rock and they lay there, feeling the sun warm upon their faces, aware of the nearness of each other. Max touched her cheek, and the contact was a caress. Then his fingers ran gently through her hair and she turned impulsively and kissed the palm of his hand. It was a spontaneous gesture, a declaration, telling herself as much as it told him.

'You're sweet, Tessa. I've known it all along. I sensed it right at the beginning, beneath that prickly disguise.'

She had no disguise now.

★ ★ ★

No one can afford to rest too long on a climb. Even in foothills the light can suddenly change, leading climbers astray. It was now far into the afternoon and the peaks above were shrouded in mist. Soon it could engulf them. Max drew her to her feet reluctantly and they abseiled down the face of a rocky overhang to a twenty-foot-wide ledge of scree below, then he coiled in the rope. The day's climbing was over, but the enjoyment lingered with them.

To one side of the path a narrow ribbon of grassy earth slanted down to the lower slopes, the easy slopes which culminated in the valley. It was their last moment together and neither wanted it to end. They began to walk down slowly, and in the distance Tessa saw the glint of Kerstin's blonde head in the slant of the evening sun. She was sitting on a small outcrop of rock, with Steve beside her. Max slowed.

'There's plenty of time,' he said. 'No need to hurry. We can have this last stretch to ourselves, at least.'

Her pleasure was unreasonable; a tremulous delight. The others were too far away to have seen or heard them and a moment later the path curved, cutting them completely from view. Max slid an arm round her waist as they walked on, drawing her to his side, and the contact renewed that surging delight.

There was laughter in his voice as he said, 'What made you hold out on me like that? Why did you pretend you knew nothing about climbing? What were you trying to punish me for?'

'I don't know. Nothing. I was stupid.'

He laughed. 'You were indeed. I saw at first glance that you knew the game and had been well taught. Who was your tutor?'

'My father.'

'He was a climber?'

'A famous one. His books on climbing have been published all over the world. You must have heard of James Pickard.'

Max stood still abruptly, and she was shocked by his face. It had turned hard as stone.

His arm fell away.

'*What* name did you say?'

'James Pickard,' she repeated, and a cold tongue of fear licked her heart for now there was no warmth left in this man.

'Is that your name — Pickard? Why did you pretend it was Richard?'

'I didn't. It was a mistake made on my boarding card by the ticket clerk at Bergen.'

'Why didn't you correct it?'

'I couldn't be bothered. I didn't think it important.' Bewilderment and alarm were in her voice.

'Is that why you didn't correct me when I called you Miss Richard?'

'Yes. I didn't think we'd ever meet again, so what did it matter?'

'And when you found my home and walked right in — why didn't you enlighten me then?'

'What do you mean — enlighten you? You just called me Tessa and made no formal introductions, so my surname was never mentioned. It just never came up. Besides, I'd forgotten. What did you expect me to say?' She gave a bewildered laugh. "I'm sorry, but the other day you thought my name was Richard, but it isn't, it happens to be Pickard, so I'm a fraud and I think you ought to know'?' She laughed. 'By that time I'd completely forgotten about the mistaken identity, and I can't see that it matters.'

The little tongue of fear probed more deeply as Max burst out, 'Not *matter?* Good God, if I'd known who you were I would never have welcomed you into my home. I would have shown you the door.'

'But why — *why?*'

He went right on, as if he hadn't even

heard. 'Now I understand a lot of things. Your attitude to me right from the start. Hiding in your cabin. Assuming another name. Even your pretence today, trying to kid me you knew nothing about climbing. But that was where your act fell apart because experienced climbers can never hide their experience. I don't know what you're here for, but so long as you are, keep out of my way, you beautiful bitch.'

Shaking with anger, she gasped, 'I don't know what you're talking about!'

'Like hell you do. Like hell you know that your father tried to kill mine, up there on the glacier.'

8

After the first horrified moment she cried, 'That's a lie — a damnable lie! My father would be incapable of such a thing!'

Max was walking away, his heavy climbing boots crunching on the rough earth. She stumbled after him, grabbed his arm and whirled him round.

'Take back what you said. *My father was never a murderer.*'

'He tried his best to be.' The voice was hard, incisive, with a bitter edge, then he shook her off with a movement which was both contemptuous and violent, and she watched his implacable figure stride away. It was useless to follow. She could only remain where she was, feeling sick and shaken, outraged that such an accusation should be made against her father of all people, and for some reason the fact that it came from Max Hyerdal made it a hundred times worse. She could never forgive it. This forged a breach between them which was incapable of healing, but before God she vowed to prove him wrong and to stay until she did, no matter how long it took.

She would remain in this quiet, serene, seemingly innocent place until this man's terrible slander against James Pickard was removed once and for all.

She looked down the mountainside and saw the valley sleeping peacefully below. The fjord was calm and clear and on the fir-clad slopes the picturesque Norwegian houses looked as simple and friendly as always, but at least one of them sheltered a liar. More than one, because if Max believed this story about her father, then others did too. The embittered Lars Hyerdal for one, and the writer of the anonymous letter for another.

The unpalatable thought struck her that Max himself might have written that note, but, angry as she was, it was hard to believe. He wasn't a vindictive man — or did she believe that merely because she wanted to? As a person he had baffled her from the start. His character was complex and one which she would never understand. Right at this moment she didn't want to. She was incapable of analysing or questioning or even reasoning. She could only think of him as hard and unfeeling. Those moments of tenderness which had meant so much to her had meant nothing at all to him; as abruptly as he had turned to her, he had turned away.

It was then that another realisation hit her. Not once had she spared a thought for Dan. She hadn't even remembered him as she kissed Max Hyerdal, returning passion for passion, desire for desire, aware only that this feeling was not sexual alone but went deeper than anything she had experienced before with any man. She had a lot in common with Dan Delaney; she liked and respected him, had learned to depend on him and in many ways to be led by him, but that was as far as it went.

She remembered her moment of rebellion when he ordered her father's school sign to be removed, and her refusal to acknowledge the impulse which had prompted it, because to do so would be to admit that in Dan there was a hard core of calculation and ambition. She admitted it now, admitting also that, heaven help her, she had fallen in love with a man far more ruthless, far less admirable. She watched Max's broad, retreating back and heard his heavy footfall increase in speed as he headed in Kerstin's direction — impatient to get to her and away from herself. Tessa thought wryly that he need not have hurried; she was too shaken to move.

'Tessa, where are you?'

It was Steve. She couldn't call back because

her throat was taut and dry, but she made a supreme effort and walked on. Rounding a bend she saw Steve coming to meet her and Max and Kerstin rapidly disappearing down the slope, heading towards the hotel. Her hand was in his and even at such a moment as this Tessa wondered whether the girl had put it there, or whether he had taken hold of it; even at this distance they seemed to walk as lovers walk, aware only of themselves.

'Max was in a helluva hurry,' Steve said as he joined her. 'Funny chap — sometimes I can't get the hang of him. Perhaps it's the result of having a temperamental artist for a father — although God knows Max gets away on his cargo ships often enough, and, from all one hears, lives it up in Bergen and elsewhere. Mainly with Kerstin, I suspect, but there are probably others. He has an eye for women.'

Tessa knew that. She also knew about his relationship with Kerstin because the Norwegian girl had openly hinted at it when they first met, but she didn't want to think about it or discuss it. She didn't want to think about Max in any way at all, but his voice pronouncing its dreadful accusation against her father pounded mercilessly on her brain. '*Your father tried to kill mine . . .* '

Up there on the glacier; far away up there

on the frozen ceiling of the world. She lifted her head and scanned the lofty peaks, but no glimpse of that sea of ice could be seen from here. It was a lost world, silent, remote, guarding its secrets, but somehow, some day, in some way she would wrench the truth from its frozen heart. It was a wild and impossible vow, but she made it and meant it. '*Do you remember the Jostedal Glacier?*' the anonymous note had asked. Now it was her turn to ask a question. What did the glacier remember?

'I've spoken to you three times and you haven't heard a word,' Steve said reproachfully.

She jerked to attention. 'I'm sorry. What did you say?'

'Merely that you had us all fooled. You climb like an expert.' He gave a sudden laugh. 'Maybe that's why Max was in such a fury just now, marching downhill like the wrath of God. What happened up there?'

'Nothing — except, as you say, that he realised I'd fooled him.'

'What made you?'

She shrugged and answered vaguely, 'Oh, I don't know. Just the general assumption that I didn't know a thing about climbing, I expect.'

But it wasn't entirely that. It was Kerstin's

taunt the day they had met in Voss, coupled with Max's insistence upon teaching her; the two combined had been a challenge. Tessa couldn't understand now why she had played such a childish trick, but surprising him had given her great satisfaction. She had enjoyed it, and so had he. They had laughed together . . . they had kissed . . .

Abruptly, she ran down the last stretch and Steve called: 'Hey! What's the hurry?' and came in pursuit, taking hold of her and slowing her down. 'Haven't you had enough activity for one day?' He slipped an arm about her waist and said persuasively, 'Don't let's catch up with the others. Let 'em go.'

His honest face smiled into hers, revealing quite clearly how much he liked her. Thank God for Steve, she thought. Thank God for someone I can trust.

They lapsed into a leisurely stroll, delaying their return, reaching the hotel some fifteen minutes after the others. Tessa was thankful to discover they were not in sight.

'How about a drink?' Steve suggested.

'Sounds lovely. I could do with one.'

They dumped their gear on the wooden verandah and shed their climbing boots. It was an unwritten law of the hotel that fishermen and climbers left their equipment outside and didn't mar the pine floors with heavy footwear. One corner of the verandah had become a general dumping ground and they added to it. After she had shed her rucksack Tessa's hand slid automatically to the zipped pocket in which she had put the anonymous note; wherever she went, that went too. She felt the crisp paper and the touch re-sparked the anger which had inflamed her up there on the mountainside — the anger, and the shock, and the pain of hearing such an accusation from a man she loved and hated, two emotions dangerously akin.

They were turning towards the bar when the sound of a motor launch cut through the evening air. 'That must be Max and Kerstin,' Steve said, glancing towards the fjord. Against her will she did the same and saw the dim outline of a launch gliding away from the jetty, the gathering dusk revealing two shadowy figures aboard. She recognised Max's broad shoulders and the shape of his head, also the sound of Kerstin's laughter as it came echoing across the water.

'Good,' said Steve. 'They've gone. I was afraid they might be in the bar. Now I can have you to myself.'

As he led her inside Tessa heard the diminishing hum of the launch and suddenly her throat was taut again, so taut that when Steve asked what she would drink she jerked, 'Anything you like, but make it strong.'

Olaf, that general handyman, was serving. He saw her clothes and nodded approval. 'So you climb too, *Froken*?' Evidently this sent her up in his estimation. 'Mr. Hyerdal would be interested to know that. He's a great climber. A pity you missed him — he was in here just now.'

'Alone?' she asked, and was surprised when he nodded.

'Kerstin must have been repairing the ravages of the open air,' Steve said.

Kerstin had little need to do that, Tessa thought, and was glad they were late. To have come face to face with Max again would have been painful as well as embarrassing.

Half an hour and two whiskies later she was ready to leave. She couldn't maintain any more bright conversation and when Steve suggested dinner she sought an excuse. 'I can't go into the dining-room in these old jeans.'

'You can go to your shanty home, take a shower, and change.'

'I'll go to my shanty home, take a shower, and change into a house-coat — that's the mood I'm in. A meal on a tray and an early night. All that exercise . . . '

He was understanding, but reluctant to let her go. 'I'll walk down with you and try to make you change your mind.'

As he held the bar door open she saw the Revolds going into the dining-room with Margrit Amundsen. They exchanged greetings and, as always, Margrit's smile was friendly.

'Had a good day?' Thor asked.

'Wonderful,' Tessa said, lying through her teeth. Well, at least one part of it had been wonderful . . .

'Kerstin has been telling me what a skilled climber you are,' Margrit put in. 'You've been hiding your light under a bushel. She asked me to say goodbye if I saw you, because she has to get back to Voss tonight and couldn't wait.'

So that explained her early departure with Max — or was meant to. Tessa didn't want to think about that and exchanged good nights before going out on to the verandah to collect her gear. Steve swung her rucksack over his shoulder, took hold of her hand, and together they walked down the path through the pine trees. His nearness was comforting and when they reached her cabin she didn't discourage his kiss. It was kind and affectionate, but before any passion could enter into it she was saying good night and shutting the door.

He stayed it with his foot.

'Sure you won't change your mind?'

'Quite sure. It's been a strenuous day.'

'You can say that again — and I didn't do half of what you did. Where did you learn to climb so well?'

'Back home. My father taught me. He had a climbing school.'

She had switched on the porch light and it shone full upon Steve's face, spotlighting his surprise.

'Pickard! *James Pickard?* Is he your father?'

She said with an effort, 'He was. He died last spring.'

Surprise gave way to concern. 'Good God, Tess, I didn't know or I wouldn't have been so clumsy. Forgive me.'

'You weren't clumsy at all and there's nothing to forgive. How were you to know, all this distance away?'

Suddenly it was wonderful to speak to someone who knew of her father — someone friendly and impartial and unprejudiced.

'How did you know of him, Steve? Did you read his books?'

'I tried to once, but as you may have noticed today climbing isn't my forte. But I used to listen to his broadcasts and saw him a few times on TV — outdoor programmes and sports talks. That was when I was a sports writer and part of my job was to keep abreast of what the experts were doing and saying.'

'Did you ever meet him?' she asked eagerly.

'Once, very briefly. I was sent to interview him, but had no luck. He said he didn't like being interviewed so would I excuse him, and off he went. And off *I* went, back to the office with my tail between my legs.'

Tessa choked. This characteristic picture of James made her want to laugh and cry at the same time.

'He was like that, Steve. He didn't mean to be rude. He was basically a shy man and interviewers terrified him. Put him before a mike or a TV camera to talk about his pet subject, and he would open up, but ask him to talk about himself and he would close up like a clam . . . '

Mercifully, Steve didn't notice the way her words clipped off.

'You're rather like him, Tessa. Your father was dynamic, but unassuming. You stand out in a crowd, but you're unaware of it. Maybe that's why I like you.' He dropped a kiss on the end of her nose. 'You look tired, kiddo. I won't keep you.' With his genial smile and

105

a wave of the hand he was gone.

She shut the door and leaned against it. Why had she felt that sudden shock when remembering her father's habit of closing up like a clam when questioned about himself? He had been shy, modest, unassuming as Steve had said. This was the reason why James Pickard had been reticent about himself, not because he had something to hide.

Never that.

★ ★ ★

She didn't know when she began to feel that someone had been in her cabin. Perhaps it was when she tripped over a cushion lying upon the floor, or later when reaching for a cigarette, only to find that the packet wasn't in its usual place, but at neither time was she conscious of a definite feeling of suspicion. She wasn't a very tidy person. She scattered newspapers and magazines haphazardly, left things on chairs, dropped them around, then periodically had a good set-to and tidied the place. So a cushion tossed on to the floor was nothing unusual, although she couldn't recall dropping this particular one. Not that that meant anything. It was a habit of hers to fling cushions aside when putting her feet up for a smoke and a read.

So she picked up the cushion and tossed it on to the nearest chair, then went on to the shower, shedding her clothes as she went. They left a trail in her wake which she had to pick up later, and it was then that she missed the cigarettes. They had their special place in a niche beside the tiled Norwegian stove; she had only to reach out to get one automatically, and did so now, the bundle of discarded clothing under one arm, but her hand met only empty space. The cigarettes had gone.

Her bare foot stepped on something which crushed lightly beneath her instep and, looking down, she discovered that it was the cigarette packet, its contents scattered. Strange, she thought. I don't remember doing that.

Dumping her soiled clothes in the kitchen sink she went back and gathered up the cigarettes, deciding that she must have brushed the packet to the floor as she flew around this morning, preparing to leave. She had been very excited; unexpectedly so. No doubt that was why she had failed to notice the scattered cigarettes.

She lit one now, then sat back on her

heels and surveyed the room, which was more untidy than she realised. Time for another blitz, Tessa Pickard — just look at those scattered books! She went across and began to push them into vacant places on the shelves, and that was the moment when the first pang of suspicion really stirred. After packing her rucksack the previous night she had flicked along the bookshelves for something to read, running her finger along the titles, selecting an occasional one and putting it back until she found something which appealed — so it wasn't she who had pulled these out and flung them aside.

Tessa stood up slowly and looked carefully round the place. There were no other disturbing signs; nothing that hit her in the eye. She began to doubt her memory, to blame herself for being more scatterbrained than she realised, but as she went into the kitchen and broke eggs into a bowl she was conscious of an uneasiness which sprang into definite alarm when, reaching for the eggwhisk which was normally kept in a drawer with other kitchen tools, she found the drawer half open, as if someone had hurriedly pushed it back but not far enough.

That clinched it. She had had toast and yoghurt and fruit for breakfast. She had needed nothing from that drawer. She hadn't opened it.

A chill touched her. Drawing her towelling robe closer she walked back into the living area of the cabin and looked around. Someone *had* been here. She was certain of it. She could sense it. Nothing was drastically disturbed, but she could almost feel the movement of unseen hands hurriedly searching, riffling through easy and accessible places, pressed for time. That was why the search had been superficial; a more thorough one would have required a more thorough cover-up, but scattered cigarettes, an overturned cushion, a few books pulled out at random might very well not be noticed in the room of a not-too-tidy young woman.

She began to notice other things; small things out of place, so unimportant that at first glance she couldn't be sure whether she hadn't left them there herself. But she *was* sure. She was absolutely convinced that another person's hands had probed down the sides of chairs, felt under cushions, flicked through the leaves of books, scanned kitchen drawers, and even emptied a packet of cigarettes . . .

She picked up the crushed packet and examined it carefully. If someone had taken the trouble to empty anything so small, then the article they searched for must be even smaller. Something which could be folded and slipped inside. A piece of paper. A note.

The anonymous note, of course.

9

Her first instinct was to rush to the 'phone, call the hotel, and report the break-in. Her hand was actually on the receiver when reason intervened. A break-in had to be proved, and how could it be? The door lock was intact and showed no signs of tampering. She herself had left the window open — she clearly remembered doing so because the day promised to be warm and she hated coming home to airless rooms. The fact that the window now swung upon its hinges suggested only that she had fastened the latch inadequately. A gust of wind from the fjord could easily dislodge it and often did, leaving the window banging as it was now.

And the fact that anyone could step through that window from the tiny porch outside didn't prove that someone had actually done so. The sill was low. Either a man or a woman could easily climb through, but because the weather was dry there were no footprints. So she wouldn't be able to answer the first and most obvious question — how did she *know* there had been an intruder? Nothing was missing and only small signs, signs so negligible that they would be unconvincing to others, indicated some unseen presence.

So she hadn't much hope of being believed. She couldn't raise a hue and cry just because a packet of cigarettes had been spilled, a cushion overturned, a drawer left half open, and a few books scattered.

She pulled the window shut, fastened it, and drew the curtains. She was in no mood for eating now. She curled up on the bright Norwegian rug before the stove, lit another cigarette, and thought hard. A master key? There was one for every room in the hotel and for all outdoor accommodation. They were the head porter's responsibility and he kept them locked in a cupboard — everyone on the staff knew that. Even so, he might forget to lock the cupboard just once . . .

She dismissed the thought because logic cast doubt upon it. No member of the hotel staff would be interested in her room. She was a tourist from England who had landed herself a temporary job; she was travelling light and therefore unlikely to have anything valuable or worth stealing. So the staff could be dismissed, from Olaf down to the night porter. This break-in had been made for one reason only; she knew what that was and could narrow the suspects down to one — Max.

The answer thrust itself unwillingly into her mind, and she refused to accept it. Was it likely that a man who openly accused her father of attempted murder would be cowardly enough to send anonymous hints by mail, little poisoned darts intended to wound? Max might be many things, but he wasn't the type to whisper through keyholes. He would hurl his accusations in a person's face, as he had done up there on the mountain.

So it had to be someone else; someone who knew the story and wanted to stab James Pickard in the back. Kerstin? Why not? She was in love with Max and, like everyone in these parts, would be well acquainted with Lars Hyerdal's story. She might feel particularly vengeful against a man believed to have injured Max's father; she could have wanted to strike a blow against Pickard in support of Max's hatred of him.

All Tessa's conjectures about the one English person in particular whom Max disliked were now answered. It wasn't herself. It wasn't his mother. It was James.

The cigarette burned her hand and she dropped the stub into the hearth with a little gasp. Thought had obsessed her to such a degree that she had left the cigarette dangling between inert fingers. Now the little stab of pain was an activator, sharpening her brain. Yes, she thought, Kerstin was a distinct possibility, but what about Lars? The man was embittered and masochistic — keeping that photograph 'as a reminder' indicated that. Possibly he was vindictive too. He might well want to hurt someone who had once hurt him, but if he wrote that note, who went to Vijne to post it for him? He couldn't go alone, and Max wouldn't be likely to connive in the matter. Bitter as he felt against James, he would discourage Lars from recalling the past and definitely from contacting the man believed to have ruined his life. She remembered his protest when his father drew her attention to the photograph. It had been one of concern, possibly of anxiety because he didn't want his father to torture himself that way.

And, of course, Lars couldn't have searched her cabin. He would need an accomplice both for mailing the letter and for endeavouring to retrieve it. Kerstin might wish to ingratiate herself with him, because she hoped one day to be his daughter-in-law. The suspicion seemed reasonable, backed by the fact that Kerstin could have created the opportunity to search her cabin while Max was in the bar and she, ostensibly, in the powder room; doubtless he had revealed Tessa's true identity as they returned together after the climb and Kerstin's immediate instinct, whether she was the writer of the note or merely a tool in the hands of Lars, would be to find out if Tessa had brought it with her and, if so, to get it back.

The more Tessa thought about it, the more possible this theory seemed, if only because, apart from Max, there was no one else to suspect. And she herself had made things easy by leaving her cabin window on the latch. She could picture Kerstin climbing nimbly over the sill, moving lightly and swiftly through the place, then running back to join Max in the bar or meeting him down by the jetty. It added up. It could have worked.

Except for one thing. 'Kerstin has been telling me what a skilled climber you are,' her mother had said. So they had been talking together up there at the hotel, long enough to discuss the day's climbing and the surprise Tessa had sprung. The conversation

115

might have been only a matter of minutes, but those minutes would have eaten into the one essential factor — time.

She tried to calculate Kerstin's movements during the interval of approximately fifteen minutes between her return with Max and her own return with Steve. Her cabin was five minutes' walk through the garden; less if one ran, and Kerstin was athletic enough to run swiftly. So about five minutes at the minimum would have been swallowed by the trip to the cabin and back — provided she did rejoin Max at the hotel and not down by the jetty later. On top of that Kerstin had met her mother and had been forced to stop and talk — more precious minutes wasted. That didn't leave much time for breaking into the cabin and searching the place. No wonder it had been no more than a superficial skimming of the surface, in which case Tessa knew she could expect a return visit some time.

But all this was guesswork. Only one thing was positive — that the writer of the anonymous note now knew who she was, and what had brought her here, and was anxious to get the note back because he was afraid that sometime she would see his handwriting and recognise it, and promptly know his identity.

Once more that led right back to Kerstin. She could be alarmed because Tessa had already seen her handwriting on the hairdressing bill at Voss, and now Tessa cursed herself for not even glancing at it. She had taken it straight to the cashier and handed it in along with some kroner, picking up the change and leaving the slip of paper behind.

So perhaps everything did add up, after all. Perhaps it wasn't all guesswork, but logic. Or perhaps she was inventing all this because despite her rage she didn't want the guilty person to be Max.

★ ★ ★

Tessa ran a tired hand through her hair. She could think and reason no more. She was too distraught, not only because someone had searched her cabin, but chiefly because of Max's appalling accusation against James Pickard. No one who had ever met her father would believe it.

Had Max met him? If so, it could only have been when he was a child during the war, when Pickard served with the Snow Corps in Norway. Max's father had done the same, so it was possible they had served together, since the force was an Allied one.

117

And something had happened; something which discouraged her father from ever returning to a country of which he had always spoken with nostalgic affection — with sadness too, she had sometimes thought, and wondered why, but the reason now presented was totally out of character and totally unacceptable.

Before going to bed she stood by the window and gazed up at the shadowy peaks. What *had* happened up there on the Jostedal Glacier, that eternal ice-field which was beginning to exercise a mesmeric effect upon her? More than once she had walked to the other end of the village to see the extraordinary ice tunnel at the base of the mountain and to stare up at the overhanging shelf which looked like a gigantic step to the frozen ceiling. It was menacing, but impressive; beautiful, but threatening, as if at any moment it would come avalanching down. But despite the icy deposit at the base, proving that sometimes it did, she had never yet seen it happen.

★ ★ ★

The following Saturday a folk festival was held in Balestrand and she was pleased when Steve asked her to go with him. She hoped the event would take her mind off things for a brief time at least.

The festival was well patronised and gay, with colourful national costumes from various regions and colourful songs and dances to go with them. A stage had been set up in the open air and they sat upon the ground to watch the performers. Boats streamed down the fjord from wide-flung villages and steamers came from farther afield, until soon the place was overflowing with visitors, all highly partisan in their applause for their favourite groups.

The festival began at three and continued well into the evening, with a vast supply of food on sale in a nearby marquee. The endless variety of Norwegian dishes still amazed Tessa even after a month in the country; a whole month since she had arrived on the *Valkyrie* — that amazed her too.

'Steve, do you realise that it's four whole weeks since I came?'

'And I'm no nearer to making you fall in love with me,' he said good-humouredly. 'But I'm an optimist. Didn't you say you'd come for two months? That leaves one to go. Anything can happen in a month.'

Anything could indeed, like meeting a man you want to dislike and being wildly attracted to him instead, but that wasn't

119

the only thing to make this past month memorable. She had at least found out certain things: she knew why the anonymous note had been written, even if she didn't yet know the sender. She knew that the writer was anxious to discover whether she had brought it with her and, if so, to get it back. She knew that it referred to something important and terrible in her father's life, that Max Hyerdal was his enemy and hers also, and that she was ashamed because even so she couldn't get the man out of her mind, or forget his passion and her own leaping response. She ought to hate him. She did hate him. But she wanted him none the less.

They had not met since their mountain climb and Tessa was glad of that. She dreaded coming face to face with him and meeting nothing but coldness and dislike. All the same, she was determined to see him and face him somehow. She couldn't let him say vile things about James Pickard and get away with it. He owed an explanation, he owed the truth, and he owed her father a full retraction.

Steve had gone to refill their plates and she sat there in the sun, letting the music and the gaiety flow over her, isolated briefly in a moment of time which was untouched by anything but the happiness around her. It was impossible not to be infected by it. She sat on the grass hugging her knees, her eyes closed and her face uplifted to the sun. She was aware of the music ending, of a dance coming to a whirling finish, of a burst of enthusiastic applause — and then of a shadow moving across the sun so that its warmth was cut from her face and behind her closed eyelids was sudden darkness.

She waited for the cloud to pass, and when it failed to she opened her eyes and saw Max standing above her, his tall figure outlined against the sky.

'Enjoying yourself, Tessa Pickard?'

'I was. Until now.'

'Your father enjoyed himself in these parts too.'

'How?'

'Did he never tell you?'

'Only of how much he loved this country.'

Max's laugh was short and mirthless.

'So much that he never dared come back. Did he tell you why?'

'I'm waiting for you to do that. You made a terrible accusation against him. Explain it — and then take back every word.'

He was on the point of making an angry retort when suddenly his whole attitude changed. He looked down at her for a moment and if she had not known him better she would have thought there was compassion in his voice as he said, 'Go home, Tessa Pickard. It's all in the past. Go home.'

'I will when I've found out the truth — and more besides.'

'What more?'

'The identity of the person who wrote an anonymous letter which tipped my father over the edge of sanity into despair, and made him take his life. It was mailed from Norway, not far from this very place.'

If his back had not been turned to the sun so that she saw him only in silhouette, Tessa could have seen the expression on his face. Instead, all she saw was a stiffening of his body, but whether it was caused by surprise or sudden wariness she could not tell. Wariness, no doubt. She had put him on guard.

'I know nothing about . . . '

His voice clipped off, interrupted by Steve saying gaily, 'Second course coming up, ma'am, and a flagon of wine to wash it down.'

He dumped the replenished picnic tray upon the grass and Max turned and walked away. Tessa wanted to cry with frustration and hastily put on a huge pair of dark glasses so that Steve shouldn't witness her self-betrayal. Then she drank some wine at a gulp, but it couldn't wash away the unexpected lump in her throat.

10

She forced herself to eat while Steve healthily shovelled his food down. After a few minutes he said, 'Do you know those people over there? They're staring at you. Have been, on and off, ever since we came.'

She glanced round idly.

'They're locals, I think. I've seen them around. Shopkeepers, perhaps. They probably recognise me as a customer.'

'I should think they recognise a good many customers amongst this mob, so why pick on you? I know you're gorgeous, but from the expressions on their faces you wouldn't think it. For two pins I'd go over and ask what's biting them.'

'Nothing but gnats, I expect,' Tessa answered lightly. She wasn't really interested, but had to admit that they certainly seemed interested in her — unpleasantly so. Feeling embarrassed she turned away, but not before she sensed something behind their stares, some sort of hostility which she failed to understand.

Steve said with a grin, 'Maybe you short-changed them sometime and they're wondering if it's too late to have you arrested. Let's move, shall we?'

They carried the tray and glasses back to the refreshment tent and handed them over. A woman, one of a team of voluntary workers, accepted them with a smile which subtly changed when she saw Tessa. The woman worked in the local post office, and had always been pleasant and friendly, but now she looked away quickly and busied herself with her work, and as Tessa left the marquee she wondered why.

Outside, she forgot the incident and walked down to the fjord with Steve's arm through hers.

'Enjoying yourself, my lovely?'

'Very much indeed.'

'There's a dance tonight in the Community Hall. Care to stay on for it?'

'I'd love to!'

★ ★ ★

Later, she was to regret that decision, but right now she saw no reason for not going to a dance which was to wind up a day of festivity. As boatloads of visitors departed from the quay, Balestrand seemed to withdraw into itself again, hugging itself in pleasurable anticipation. The festival had been a success. The dance would be the same.

It was, but not for Tessa. Almost from the beginning she sensed an antipathy which she had not come up against before. People who knew her well enough by now were polite, but somehow withdrawn, and again she sensed a suppressed hostility which she put down to imagination until, during intervals between dances, she and Steve were subtly left alone. To someone so well established in this part of the world, as he was, and popular too, this sudden change of attitude was puzzling. 'What's got into everybody?' he grumbled. 'Anyone would think we'd got something contagious.'

'It isn't you, Steve. It's me.'

'What do you mean, it's you?'

'I'm being ostracised, and because you are with me you're being ostracised too. Had you brought another girl, this wouldn't have happened.'

'I don't know what the devil you're talking about.'

But she did. It was obvious that her identity was now known; the news had got around that she was the daughter of James Pickard, the man who had tried to murder Lars Hyerdal up there on the glacier, years ago. *Their* Lars Hyerdal, a man who belonged to them as she most definitely did not and never would. She was an outcast now, no longer a visitor to be made welcome.

'Take me home, will you, Steve? Get me out of here and I'll tell you the reason for all this. Believe me, I need to.'

Outside, the night air was chill. Steve took off his jacket and put it round her shoulders, saying with forced jocularity, 'Come on — confess! What've you been up to? Having an affair with the local mayor and caught in the act?'

Despite her unhappiness, Tessa laughed. 'I wish it were something so trivial.'

'Trivial!' he mocked. 'Carrying on with a respectable married man like Mayor Horsdal?' He clucked with disapproval. 'And I believed you to be a highly moral young woman!' His arm went round her in an encouraging hug. 'Come on — open up. What was all that in aid of back there? It isn't like the folk in these parts to cold-shoulder anyone.'

She took a deep breath and said, 'Not even the daughter of a would-be murderer?'

Steve stopped dead in his tracks and stared. For the first time since Tessa had met him, he was struck dumb.

'It's what they believe,' she said bitterly.

'Max Hyerdal and everyone, but why, I just don't know.'

'Hyerdal,' Steve echoed thoughtfully. 'You don't mean, you *can't* mean that it was your father who did that thing to Lars?'

'What thing?' she cried helplessly. 'All I know is that James Pickard, *my father*, is accused of trying to murder Lars Hyerdal up there on the glacier, but how, or why, I've yet to find out. You've met my father, Steve. Would *you* believe him capable of murder?'

'Never in a million years.'

He said the words emphatically. Too emphatically. So emphatically that she knew it was for her benefit. She looked at him sharply and saw that his normally carefree face was serious, guarded.

'You know something,' she said quietly. 'You know something, you've heard something . . . '

He slipped his arm through hers again and led her on towards the quay, then he handed her into his boat, saying, 'I'll tell you when we're under way.'

In a moment he had cast off and was heading towards Fjaerland Fjord. The sound of dance music followed them and to her heightened imagination the beat of it seemed angry and threatening.

She burst out, 'For God's sake, *tell* me, Steve! Tell me all you know.'

'All I know is how Lars Hyerdal was injured, not the identity of the man responsible. I've never known that, only that he was English, serving with the same mountain regiment here during the war. Was your father a member of the Allied Snow Corps?'

She nodded mutely. The lights of Balestrand were fading and with them the sullen throb of music, then there was nothing but silence and darkness, with only the lap of water and the soft stutter of the outboard motor to disturb the night.

Steve said, 'Lars was left alone on the glacier, seriously injured. His companion abandoned him.'

'Then his companion couldn't have been my father. He would never abandon a fellow-climber, except to get help.'

'Of course not. But the circumstances were — well — odd.'

'Odd? In what way?'

'I'll tell you the whole story. You know it's dangerous to cross the glacier during summer, but in wartime the seasons couldn't be considered and mountain regiments had to take risks. It was at the time of the Quisling Government and a pair of expert skiers and climbers had to cross the glacier to get an urgent message to the Freedom Fighters, who had a secret base at Vijne.'

'Vijne!'

'Could any place be more ideal for a hide-out than that isolated spot? The exercise meant crossing the glacier during the height of summer, then climbing down the mountainside beyond Fjaerland and making their way to the secret base. The Englishman arrived alone. He said that Hyerdal had sprained his ankle too severely to continue, that he had left him adequately provided for, but help was urgently needed. He gave the man's location, but when Hyerdal was eventually found it was far from the indicated spot. And he had wounds — blows — even worse, serious spinal injuries. Frankly, only a man as fit as he could have survived at all. Later, he claimed that there had been a heated dispute between them, an argument over the course they should take or something. Hyerdal was subordinate in rank, and tension must have been pretty high because the Englishman lost his temper, knocked him down, and injured him. A fall on an icy glacier can be treacherous and often fatal. The man must have known that he had injured Hyerdal seriously and that if abandoned he must die. Perhaps the man panicked. Who knows?'

Tessa burst out, 'It wasn't James Pickard! It couldn't have been!'

Steve said gently, 'I don't know who it was, Tessa. I'm merely giving you the known facts. Remember that the man misdirected the search party, which suggests that he didn't want Hyerdal to be found. And remember that Hyerdal was so badly injured that he couldn't possibly have moved. It was this that authenticated his story. A man might have shuffled a few yards with a sprained ankle, but Hyerdal was found a considerable distance from the location given by his superior officer, *and* almost mortally injured. Could he have moved himself? I ask you — could he?'

She couldn't speak. She couldn't utter a sound. They drifted along in silence for some time and at length she managed to ask, 'What happened to the Englishman?'

'All I know is that he went back home. He wasn't court-martialled or publicly disgraced. He went of his own free will and he went at once.'

'And Lars Hyerdal brought no charges against him?'

'None. It was wartime, remember, and Norway was occupied. All activities were underground by then and any kind of enquiry would have focused attention on the Freedom Fighters. It would have been a useful betrayal to the enemy.'

The boating island was in sight. Steve tied up and helped her ashore, then he put his arms round her and said compassionately, 'You poor kid — you've walked right into it, haven't you? These people think the world of Lars Hyerdal. He is a hero to them and they've never never forgotten the crime against him. I hate to say this because I hate the thought of losing you, but you'd be wise to clear off home and you'd certainly be a great deal happier.'

'*Happier*? Knowing there are people in the world who believe my father capable of such a thing? Let them be as hostile to me as they like — I'm staying right here until I prove them wrong.'

Steve kissed her gently.

'My poor sweet,' he said, 'you can't win. You haven't a hope.'

11

During the following days Tessa sought refuge in work, determined to keep her mind so occupied that there was no room for thought. Off duty she took long and energetic walks to the far reaches of the village and the region of the overhanging glacier. Its mesmerism was now doubled; she couldn't keep away; she was drawn to it, not by a morbid desire for self-torture, but by a feeling that its imponderable silence harboured answers to questions which only the glacier could yield.

She would gaze up at it, studying it, memorising every line and projection. Outlined like some crystalline monster against the sky, the craggy mountainside below looked like a wrinkled face beneath a gigantic and frozen eyelid. It could be climbed, that craggy face, despite the ice-floes running down to the frozen hillock with its deep tunnel at the foot. She was convinced it could be climbed. There was an approach far to the right, away from the ice-floes and the huge deposit, which would enable a climber to 'traverse in' and reach the summit within two or three days if the route was negotiated carefully and mapped out well beforehand.

Something sparked inside her, a questing eagerness to explore, a response to challenge. Whatever it was, it was a spur and she began to visit the place more frequently, armed with a pair of binoculars bought at the hotel shop. She took charting paper and spent hours sketching the mountain face in detail. The binoculars revealed at least three good spots for overnight bivouacs and a horizontal series of movements which would make a convenient traverse. At the same time they exposed an unsuspected crossing of snow and ice, which apparently lay there all the year round, in which case she knew they must lie in diagonal traverse and represent danger. They might even conceal a wind-slab, formed by wind-blown snow which had settled insecurely on top of old, its crust hard but unstable, ready to break off easily.

She marked these danger spots and carefully began a plan of campaign, although she would not acknowledge even to herself why she did so. To attempt such a climb alone would be madness.

But not impossible. Not if one went about it the right way, navigation carefully mapped out beforehand.

Planning a climbing route seemed to bring

her near to her father again. As a child she had spent hours watching him do this, measuring almost to within a foot the safest and yet most interesting way to tackle a rock-face. Even then she had been taught how to recognise vee-chimneys and upstanding 'flakes' suitable for belaying, and later how to use a slide rule to calculate measurements. She could do a reasonably expert job at it now and set about it diligently, returning many times to make revisions, telling herself that she only did so to keep thought at bay and to avoid people.

Up to a point this was true, for despite her vow to defy local prejudice and to hold her head high, she found it wasn't easy to assume nonchalance when enduring indignation and heartache. She worked at her job as usual, behaved as usual, carried on the normal pattern of living, but knew all the time that she was only going through the motions. She felt the whole world must see through her pretence, but only Steve knew that anything was wrong. Thoughtfully, he made no reference to it, but took her sailing whenever he was free, swam with her in the sharp waters of the fjord, and in general acted as an emotional prop for which she was grateful.

But despite all this she had to face up to

things alone and she was cowardly enough to avoid going into Balestrand. The place was the centre for local gossip, the place where she had been ostracised at the festival dance, and although she insisted to herself that she didn't care, she wasn't going out of her way to court humiliation again.

At the same time she didn't delude herself that gossip hadn't spread farther afield by now. Whether Thor or Carlota had heard this latest piece she had no idea, but if so they gave no sign. She knew Steve wouldn't tell them, and they had not attended the dance that night, nor had their friend Margrit Amundsen, but some of the hotel staff had not only been there but came from Balestrand families. Tessa couldn't hope that her identity wasn't universally known now. She even imagined, as she walked through Fjaerland village, that some knowledgeable and faintly hostile glances came her way and that even the friendly boat-builders, plying their ancient tools as they carved Viking prows to their crafts, now looked at her with either curiosity or reserve.

Every time she walked to the foothills beneath the glacier she had to pass through the village and it didn't take long to realise that her suspicion was correct. The warmth had gone out of local friendliness; people were polite, but distant. She no longer felt at home, and this sudden realisation made her aware of how quickly she had originally been accepted. Demonstrative friendliness was not part of the native character, but she had been made welcome. Now the welcome was gone, and for the first time she obtained a real glimpse of her father's suffering when public opinion had turned against him over the Wynyard affair.

One is never so alone as in unhappiness, for no one can share one's inner isolation except someone deeply loved and who reciprocates to such a degree that out of that love comes total understanding, the *rapport* which makes two people one. There had been no one to play that rôle in James Pickard's life. There was no one in hers. Dan wasn't around to turn to, and if he had been she knew well enough what his advice would be — return to England and forget the whole thing. In short, Dan would wash his hands of it, intent only on his own affairs, his own ambitions. For this reason she couldn't even write to him, and didn't want to. It came as something of a surprise to realise that she scarcely even thought of him now.

There was only Steve, who believed, as she had done with her father, that he knew what she was going through, but never having gone through it himself hadn't really the faintest idea. Equally, she realised now that despite her closeness to James she had had little comprehension of what he thought or felt or suffered during his last unhappy days. She was his daughter and he had loved her, but she had been too young to be the recipient of a middle-aged man's grief. Even so, he had at least known that she was the one person in the world who really felt for him and cared about him, because during the enquiry and throughout the intervening days before his death they had spent nearly every moment together. They hadn't talked much, but perhaps by merely being there she had helped him to feel less alone.

She was remembering this as she trekked back to the hotel one day, armed with binoculars and slide scale and charting paper. In her new self-isolation she found herself thinking of James more and more and, inevitably, of his marriage to her mother, and she wondered now, as she had wondered always, what extraordinary impulse had made a quiet, deliberate man like her father marry in haste. The story of his whirlwind pursuit of Ruth was one of her mother's favourites, oft repeated at bridge and cocktail parties.

'He'd been in England only three weeks when he met me. It was at the house of friends. James had just returned from Norway and they were trying to get him to talk about it, but he wouldn't. He just kept looking at me the whole evening and when he took me home he suddenly asked me to dine with him the next night. My *dears*, I could hardly believe it — I'd thought him one of those strong silent heroes from ancient movies, incapable of whirlwind wooings. But within a month he had swept me off my feet!'

It had been a glamorous story to tell and being the wife of a well-known figure had also been glamorous in its way. Ruth would unconsciously preen whenever James appeared on a TV screen, even though she was bored by his subject. But there was no preening when he fell from his pedestal. Only anger.

What else had her father gone through before Tessa was even born? What desperate emotion had driven him to attack Lars Hyerdal up there in that frozen world? *If* it was true. Part of it might well be, but not all. He had a strong temper, but never lost it blindly; the provocation had to be great. She could accept that he had struck a man, but not that he would then abandon him in conditions bad enough to kill. James Pickard wasn't like that. A fighter, yes. A killer, no.

★ ★ ★

The hotel was now fully booked and life was mercifully busy. The permanent receptionist remained in Oslo and Tessa was kept hard at it, likewise Steve. His schedule left scarcely a break for meals.

'Now you know why I'm glad I don't live in the hotel,' he said one evening, as he detached himself politely but firmly from a persistent couple who saw no reason why he shouldn't be prepared to give them a sailing lesson jointly, two for the price of one, and at a moment's notice. 'If I did, people like that would be banging on my door regardless.'

'They'll be even more furious if they see me go sailing with you this evening,' Tessa said, aware of the glowering couple.

'Let them. This time it's for love.' He linked his arm in hers with a possessiveness which was becoming automatic, and she knew it was unreasonable to resist. Many a girl would be glad to be possessed by Steve; many made it obvious. He was blatantly pursued by young female guests and equally blatantly by older women too. So what was wrong with her that whenever she looked at his handsome face it became superimposed by a lean, hewn, older one? One she had every reason to hate.

140

She hadn't seen Max since their brief encounter at the folk festival. Neither he nor Kerstin had been present at the dance, but obviously he had wasted no time in broadcasting her identity to the neighbourhood. The cruelty of that cut deep. He had hurt her sufficiently up there on the mountain, without making sure that others hurt her too. Oh yes, she hated him all right, not merely because of the sudden ostracism but because of his abominable accusation against James and his abrupt command to keep out of his way. '*You beautiful bitch . . .*' It should be easy to hate a man who spared neither his words nor his punches. It *was* easy. Hatred surged up whenever she thought of him, but it made things no more bearable. All it did was tear her up inside and, ironically, remember all the more vividly their preceding moments together.

Steve had booked this sailing evening a couple of days ago. 'To make sure you're free,' he'd said, knowing full well she would be. Invitations weren't likely to come her way any more, and he knew it, and was obviously trying to convince her otherwise.

'Of course I'll be free,' she had said. 'You know that, so why pretend?'

He had playfully punched her on the nose and said, 'It's a date then, and don't duck it.

You're wandering off on your own too much these days. Don't think I haven't seen you, going off on your solitary walks. It's a bad thing, honey. Pack it up.'

He was right and she knew it, but he didn't know what she was doing out there beyond the village beneath the shadow of the glacier. As for herself she wouldn't admit *why* she was doing it, for of course she hadn't the slightest intention of attempting that crazy climb. What object would it serve? Where would be the sense? What would she see if she did reach the summit? Nothing but a vast world of ice, petrified and soundless, unable to yield up any secrets. So why this persistent desire to get up there and stare at it? Come to your senses, girl. You can't do it and you won't do it, so forget it.

★ ★ ★

She prepared a quick supper of omelettes followed by fruit and cheese and coffee, for they were both eager to get out on to the water, then Steve went down to the boating island to get his latest Enterprise ready. As she showered and donned sailing kit, Tessa suddenly remembered that other occasion when she had scattered clothes behind her across the floor and, later, recognised signs

142

of intrusion. There had been no sign of any trespasser since. She even wondered if she had imagined the whole thing; nevertheless she fastened all windows firmly and made sure the door was locked before going to join Steve. This had become an automatic ritual since that day, but as she stepped off the porch some impulse made her go back and open the window, leaving it on the latch as before. Perhaps the intruder had made no further visit because she had effectively barred his way and he was too wise or too wily to leave visible signs of a break-in. Suddenly she wanted to know if he would try again, so she left the window open as a challenging invitation, zipping the anonymous note within an inner pocket of her waterproofs.

Leaving the cabin again she came face to face with Carlota. The meeting was a surprise, for the woman never strolled down this way and never visited the staff cabins unless invited. But there she was, coming along the path leading directly to Tessa's door.

She gave her wide, frank smile and said, 'I'm glad I caught you — I came to ask a favour.'

'Of me?'

'You sound surprised. Why?'

Tessa could hardly say, 'Because I'm the last person around here that people want to bother with now,' so she just stood there uncertainly. Carlota promptly turned towards the boating island, realising from her clothes where Tessa was bound.

'Are you happy here, Tessa?' She put the question abruptly.

'Of course — very happy. Why shouldn't I be?'

'I wondered, that's all, because during these last few days you seem to have — withdrawn. There's nothing wrong, is there?'

'Not a thing.'

'I'm glad. You would tell me if there were, wouldn't you?' When Tessa didn't answer she added in a disappointed tone, 'Ah — I can see you wouldn't. Why not?'

'Why should I? *If* anything were wrong, I would cope with it.'

'You're too independent. Are all British girls like you? And is this a sample of British reserve? You're refusing to open up with me, aren't you?'

Tessa looked at Carlota's honest face and was tempted. Perhaps it would do her a power of good to confide in another woman, especially one as detached and impersonal and direct as this one. She would hand

144

out straight-from-the-shoulder talk; honest advice. All the same, Tessa resisted.

'What was this favour?' she asked.

Carlota didn't exactly shrug her shoulders in despair, but somehow implied that she wanted to.

'Simply this. Would you go to Balestrand for me tomorrow morning? The office can get by with one receptionist on duty instead of two. Olaf will take you and bring you back.' When Tessa hesitated she added, 'The trip will do you good. You haven't been anywhere or done anything for days, except go for solitary walks.'

'Plus sailing and swimming,' Tessa pointed out drily.

'And I know what *that* tone implies. 'Does everyone around here spy on what I do?'' Her voice was indulgent and amused. 'The answer is yes. Everybody knows everything that everybody does. What other entertainment is there in a place so off the beaten track? You mustn't mind.'

'Of course I'll go to Balestrand for you,' Tessa said, not wanting to go in the least, but a refusal was impossible and would require an explanation. 'What do you want me to do there?'

'Simply call at the shipping office with a

list of supplies. They bring stuff back for us from Bergen.'

'Hyerdal's, you mean?'

'Yes.'

Now why, just *why*? Tessa wondered. Taking supply lists to Hyerdal's was Olaf's job, so why ask her?

Carlota smiled blandly. 'Thanks a lot, Tessa. I'll have it made out tonight so it will be ready first thing. I see Steve's waiting for you — have a good trip.'

With a wave of the hand she turned back to the hotel, leaving Tessa puzzled. This request was no 'favour' — this was an order, something she was determined upon, something deliberately thought up. To make Tessa face people despite their attitude — was that it? If so, it meant that she had heard about the ostracism and was telling her to hold up her head and ignore it. She was forcing her to visit the place where it had all begun, not because she wanted to expose her to it again, but because she condemned it, and this was her way of telling Tessa to do the same. She was on her side. She was a friend.

Tessa went on towards the boating island and had rounded a corner when the sound of Carlota's returning footsteps made her go back to meet her. The woman must have forgotten something, something she wanted to say. But Tessa was wrong. As she turned the corner again she was just in time to see Carlota once more turn down the path leading directly to her cabin.

12

The wind came straight towards them as they sailed towards the wide stretch of the Sojne. This meant tacking and a slower approach to the open waters where Steve wanted to put his new Enterprise through her paces. Tessa had had several crewing lessons from him by now and was able to cope adequately without betraying that her mind wasn't wholly on the job. She was wondering why Carlota had gone back to her cabin the moment she was out of sight, and if her excuse of coming to ask a favour had been hastily thought up. If so, all Tessa's assumptions were incorrect and the possibility that Carlota might be the person who had searched her place, and whom she had fully expected to return, was shocking in its impact.

Like her husband, Carlota Revold had been kindness itself, and why should she, of all people, be anxious to recover an anonymous letter? What was more to the point, why should she write it in the first place — if, of course, she had? Tessa could see no possible reason and no possible connection between

Carlota Revold and the Hyerdal affair — but what about her husband? She might be acting for him . . .

She shouted above the wind, 'How long have the Revolds lived around here, Steve?'

'I've no idea. Why?' he yelled back, and immediately went into a sharp tack which meant that she had to adjust the jib quickly, pulling on the sheets until the sail filled out again.

The manœuvre over, she called in reply, 'I just wondered, that's all.'

The breeze was booming softly in the jib and she could feel the vibration right along the sheets into her hands.

'Wondered what?'

'How long they've lived here. Carlota in particular.'

'Lee-o!' Steve shouted, and tacked again, and again she had to wait until they were on course.

'Carlota?' he echoed then. 'I believe she was from Stavanger originally, but came to these parts when she married Thor. He's a native.'

Thor. How old would he be? Thirty-nine, perhaps. Not old enough to be a contemporary of Lars or to serve beside him in the Forces — but in the Freedom Fighters? They'd used youngsters, hadn't they?

Teenagers fired with enthusiasm and hero-worship. He could have hero-worshipped Lars Hyerdal and probably did, like everyone else around here. A firy young teenager fighting in the underground movement; a furious young teenager vowing vengeance on a man who tried to kill his hero. He could grow up with a desire to strike back; he could nurse it throughout the years, a festering resentment seizing upon an eventual outlet. Any outlet. Even an anonymous note could satisfy a feeling of retaliation.

They went into their last tack and sailed out into the vast Sojne. Steve shouted an order for the mainsail to be hoisted and while he turned the boat to meet the eye of the wind and hold steady, Tessa let go the jib and scrambled to the boom, hauling on the mainsail sheets with all her strength until the sail ran up and the boom swung out straight and firm.

Steve said, 'Well done — and now for Balestrand.'

'Why Balestrand?' Tessa asked as she went back to the stern and grabbed the jib sheets as well, running one length of the mainsail sheet round a jamming cleet for a better pull as Steve turned and the sails filled.

'I've some fishing tackle to pick up. There's an old man there who does repairs for me.'

He let the Enterprise go at a pelting pace. They had the full force of a driving wind behind them and reached Balestrand in no time, cruising gently towards the small yachting harbour as Tessa hauled in the sails.

'Coming with me?' Steve asked as he tied up.

Tessa was content to wait, and as he went striding off to the old man's cottage she strolled along the quayside towards larger ships at anchor. Most belonged to the Hyerdal Line and one was preparing to sail. It wasn't until she came alongside that she saw *Valkyrie* on the ship's bows, and promptly turned back. Out of the corner of her eye she saw the skipper talking to one of the crew and prayed he had not seen her. It was an effort to restrain an impulse to hurry until his step sounded close behind. She knew it well and promptly increased her pace, hoping to reach the yachting harbour before he caught up. The Enterprise sat low beneath the harbour wall and if she made it in time Max might pass above without observing her.

'I shouldn't hurry,' his voice said, 'I can outstride you, and you know it.'

He was close to her shoulder and the next moment right alongside. 'Still sticking around?' he taunted. 'Even after the other night? I heard what you had to face.'

'Thanks to *you*. You've certainly made sure that everyone for miles around knows who I am.'

He flung back, 'If you think me capable of that, you think me capable of anything.'

'I do think you capable of anything. Lies, slander — I'd put nothing past you.'

His grip on her arm was rough, and when she tried to jerk away it tightened.

'I can't make up my mind whether you're plain pig-headed or a stupid fool, Tessa Pickard. Why the hell should I tell anyone who you are?'

'To hit back at me, just as you wanted to hit back at my father. You wanted to make me suffer as he did. Sorry to disappoint you — I don't give a damn how much people ostracise me, or what *you* think of me.'

'That's obvious, otherwise you would have taken my advice and gone home. I knew how people would react if they found out who you were.'

'*When* they found out, you mean — making sure they did.'

He pulled her round, and shook her.

'Why in the name of heaven I bother with you, I don't know, but I swear I didn't tell a soul.'

'I don't believe it. People could only have found out through you or Kerstin. I'm sure you wasted no time in telling *her*.'

He released her impatiently.

'Go ahead and believe what you like. Stick your neck out. Go for your solitary walks and think up whatever fanciful ideas you care to. Don't imagine I haven't seen you wandering about alone out there beyond Fjaerland village. I'm a climber, remember. From the mountains one can see for miles and if you'll take my advice . . . '

'Which I won't.'

He gave up. 'Then I won't waste it. Just answer one question . . . '

But what that question was she was never to know, for Steve appeared, carrying a bundle of rods.

'Here comes the devoted Hatton,' Max said. 'I won't keep you two apart.'

He turned and went back to his ship, and as Steve and Tessa sailed away they saw *Valkyrie* slowly pulling away from her moorings. Tessa couldn't watch. She looked towards the distant mountains instead because suddenly all her enjoyment of the evening had gone.

★ ★ ★

153

Well, at least, she thought gladly as the hotel launch sped towards Balestrand next morning, she wasn't likely to bump into Max in the shipping office — that was one thing to be glad of. The other was that Carlota had a simple explanation for going to her cabin, and had volunteered it quite naturally when Tessa collected the order for Hyerdal's.

'I hope the rain didn't get in through your window last night? After we'd parted I remembered a storm was forecast and that you'd left your window on the hook, so I went back and closed it in case you didn't return in time. I couldn't lock it, but I made it as firm as possible.'

Tessa was grateful and said so, for they had sailed as far as Eseboten and been caught in a downpour which lasted the whole way home. But for Carlota's forethought there would have been a pool on the floor of her cabin. The realisation made her feel guilty, for when she had arrived back and seen the window pushed to, her mind had leapt to the inevitable conclusion that someone had broken in, and who could it be but Carlota, since she had actually seen the woman coming here? Tessa had made a thorough search of the place but found nothing unusual, nothing out of order, not the least sign of disturbance. But even then suspicion had not been stilled because Carlota had known that she and Steve had gone sailing for the evening. She had had plenty of time to remove all traces.

Now, of course, Tessa felt ashamed. Carlota had been kind and friendly in many unobtrusive ways ever since her arrival, and so had Thor, so how could she possibly imagine those things about him, or suspect his wife of trying to recover an anonymous letter in order to protect him? Like everything else, it had all been guess-work. She was beginning to see bogeys everywhere, in everybody, but not, thank God, in Steve. He was the one person she could be absolutely sure of because he had been a child in faraway England when Lars Hyerdal was crippled for life on the Jostedal Glacier, and Steve could have no possible motive for wanting to hurt James Pickard.

★ ★ ★

When they tied up at Balestrand Tessa told Olaf she would return in about an hour, that gave her time to hand in the order and then do some shopping. There was nothing she particularly needed, but she was determined not to hide from people who had cold-shouldered her. She would go out of her way to face them instead, challenging them with indifference.

She had forgotten that Margrit Amundsen worked for the Hyerdal Line until meeting her in the company's office. It was a typical shipping building near the quay, with an enquiry desk and a general office beyond where the clerks worked. When Tessa handed in the order, the girl at the enquiry desk asked her to wait, and it was then that Margrit came through the door of an inner room with a sheaf of papers in her hand. She looked business-like and efficient in her usual tailored suit.

She saw Tessa at once and smiled in welcome. Perhaps gratitude for this unexpected show of friendship, in a place which now withheld it, made the smile seem even warmer than it was, coupled with the fact that normally Margrit was a withdrawn sort of person, not given to smiling very spontaneously or greeting anyone with effusion. Nevertheless she walked quickly down the inner office and invited Tessa inside.

'You'll stay and have coffee with me?'

They chatted about generalities while waiting for the coffee and Tessa admired her light and airy office with its wonderful view of the fjord.

'It's even better upstairs. I have a flat there — it goes with the job. I have a lot to thank the Hyerdals for.'

Tessa remembered Carlota's opinion that Margrit demonstrated her gratitude too much, but thought this inevitable in the circumstances. She was a widow and a needy one — or had been until Hyerdal provided her with this secure job. In such conditions any woman would be anxious not to lose it. There couldn't be many such jobs in a place like Balestrand.

Seated behind her large pine desk Margrit was more relaxed than Tessa had ever seen her. She had authority here, and this obviously gave the woman confidence. They talked long after they had finished coffee — about Kerstin, inevitably, but about other things too. Tessa's temporary job at the hotel, her progress with sailing lessons, her ability as a climber.

'Kerstin was full of admiration, and Max too said how good you were.'

Nice of him, Tessa thought bitterly, and changed the subject.

'Carlota said the order was for supplies from Bergen, but it will have to wait now, I suppose?'

'Not long. A ship sails this afternoon — they're loading now, as you can see.'

157

Margrit nodded towards the window and Tessa saw a cargo vessel tied up, with cattle being hoisted aboard. She was amused by the animals' antics and their instant docility once they knew there was no way out. 'That is bound for Bergen,' Margrit continued, 'so you can tell Carlota it will bring her supplies back.'

'I thought *Valkyrie* did the Bergen run. I travelled on her from there.'

'She sailed for Trondheim last night. The vessels don't stick to the same route schedule, but are re-delegated for each voyage, according to requirements. A cargo of timber from Finland, for instance, needs a larger vessel than a few head of cattle. *Valkyrie* sailed north to collect whale-meat to be taken from Trondheim to Stavanger. You really must visit Trondheim before you return to England. You'll see the Midnight Sun, and if you stop off for a week you can explore further inland and see Laplanders with their reindeer herds, then you can return on the next cargo ship. We must persuade the Revolds to let you go.'

'It sounds wonderful. And thank you for the coffee — and the welcome.'

Margrit held out her hand. 'I'm glad you came — truly glad. Do please come to visit me any time you're in Balestrand. We've never had a chance to talk before. I hope we shall again.'

Tessa hoped so too. She left with a light heart, aware that she had made a friend. Whatever Margrit had heard, and by now she must have heard everything, it made no difference to her. She didn't sit in judgement on people — hadn't Carlota said so when relating the story of Nina Hyerdal? Tessa had liked the sound of Margrit then and she liked her even better now. As she went about her shopping she felt happier than she had felt for days, so much so that she scarcely heeded the attitude of shop-keepers. One told her frigidly that they 'were out of stock' without even bothering to check; others served her either with ill grace or frigid politeness, but none of this mattered. She had friends. Steve and the Revolds and now Margrit. She could thumb her nose at the rest.

13

A few days later she decided to visit Vijne again. She wanted to find the house used as headquarters by the Freedom Fighters, the house to which her father had come after his long trek across the ice. She lived with the story now; everything she did was motivated by it.

So on her half-day she caught the bus from Fjaerland and headed for the remote village. Vijne was so isolated that only one bus went there morning and afternoon. She caught the afternoon one, which then waited for a couple of hours before making the return journey. Vijne was apparently the end of nowhere — an ideal place for an underground movement, concealed as it was by mountains, its only approach being the narrowing strip of water which marked the end of the Fjaerland Fjord, or the winding, bumpy road which was little more than a track and which the local authorities didn't think worth repairing.

Tessa was struck once again by the desolation of this forgotten place. Nearly all the houses seemed to be unoccupied, their shuttered windows peering through overgrown trees, like sightless eyes. To which one had her father trekked on that tragic day, and how could she find out? The obvious thing was to find some talkative shop-keeper, preferably a middle-aged or elderly one who had lived here all his life and would remember those war-time years, but neither the local greengrocer nor pastry-cook understood a word of English, so she finished up with a kilo of oranges and some sticky buns she didn't want.

Then her luck turned. The only remaining shop was a kind of general store which stocked everything from soap powder to fish sold alive from tubs outside, but a corner of this shop was railed off as the local post office and behind it was a thin, grey-haired man who miraculously spoke English. What was more, he was eager to air it, not having had the opportunity for many years.

'Why not?' Tessa asked as she bought stamps. 'Lots of tourists come to this part of Norway.'

'Not to *this* place,' he said wryly. 'Only to the popular places like Balestrand or Voss, with such hotels I could never afford. So when I do journey, which is rare, I never meet English visitors, so my English it grow rusty.'

'It doesn't seem rusty to me. Where did you learn? At college? Oslo, I suppose.'

He laughed. The sound came from his throat in a dry sort of wheeze, like an instrument which hadn't been played for a long time. That was something which *had* grown rusty, she thought, shocked to realise that laughter could die of neglect.

'College — *me?* The village school gave me all my teaching, but the war — ah — that gave me more. Much more.'

'You were in the army?'

'Until Quisling collaborated, the swine. Then I join the Freedom Fighters, and the British they help us, so through them I learn their language.'

Tessa's heart leapt. This man might have met her father, might even remember him . . .

Then her excitement died. If he did remember James Pickard, he would also remember the story of Lars Hyerdal. He might even have been a member of the rescue party which went out to find him, and condemned the Englishman for giving false information as to his whereabouts and his condition. So she bit back her urgent questions and forced herself to speak casually.

'I've heard stories about the Freedom

Fighters, the things they did, their courage . . . and it all happened here, didn't it? Someone at the Nordfjord Hotel told me that Vijne was their base.'

'It was.' The man sighed nostalgically. 'Vijne really *lived* then — lived as it has never lived before or since. A quiet little place it has always been — but then, ah, the atmosphere then! The tension, the excitement, the scheming and plotting . . . there wasn't a man or boy for miles around who wasn't involved.'

'And the headquarters? Demolished, I suppose?'

'By no means! Here — I show you . . . ' He hustled to the door and pointed uphill. 'You see that house? No, not there — to the right, to the right! Between the trees, you can just see the chimneys — white they are now, but not in those days. We darkened them for camouflage and what with that and the surrounding trees no one would have suspected there was a house there. The owner cleared some of the trees after the war was over — to get a view, you understand.' He sighed again. 'Sometimes I look up at those chimneys and wish — and remember . . . '

He shook his head sadly; a man living on memories.

'Who lives there now?'

163

'Nobody. Shut up, like so many round here, except when the owners come for fishing holidays. Otherwise, who wants to come to Vijne?' He shrugged. 'Nobody. Nobody.'

Tessa glanced at her watch. There was nearly an hour before the bus left. Time to climb the hill and look at the house and return to the village to catch it? There had to be.

She was about to make excuses and get away, when a sudden thought struck her. The anonymous letter must have been posted right here; this man must have franked it with the betraying postmark, *Vijne, Norge*. She could imagine him wielding the rubber stamp and studying the letter with interest, for surely it was unusual for letters to foreign parts to be sent from this remote little place. He might even remember it — but how could she ask? 'Did anyone hand a letter across the counter to you last spring, addressed to England?' She knew it was an absurd question even as it ran through her mind.

In desperation she bought a picture postcard and sent it to Dan, saying with a little smile as she handed it over, 'I suppose you don't get many letters posted to foreign countries from here?'

He took the card, franked it, and dropped it

into the mail bag behind the counter, sparing it not so much as a glance. 'Sometimes,' he said. 'Oh yes, sometimes — when people come to open up their houses for holidays. Most of the owners come from Oslo and such places, and send letters abroad. Sophisticated folk. Too sophisticated to want to live here permanently.'

The mail bag mocked her. So did the pillar box by the shop door. The anonymous letter had probably been dropped through its gaping mouth without the man even seeing who posted it.

★ ★ ★

After all, the hill-climb wasn't time-consuming or the house so distant, but she had to keep the white chimneys in view in order to track it down, and when she finally turned along a neglected path and came suddenly face to face with it, she halted in surprise. The place had a serene, well-kept air, and the garden too was well tended. Obviously, someone kept an eye on things.

She was glad it was unoccupied because she wanted to look around. She opened the gate and it squealed faintly on its hinges. She paused with her hand on the iron latch; it was smooth and much worn. Many hands must have opened this gate, including James Pickard's. She stroked the latch with her fingers, as if trying to make contact with him. This was how it must have felt to *his* hand as he opened the gate on that fateful day. He would have been tired, spent, exhausted; perhaps he leaned upon the gate for a moment, thankful to have arrived . . .

The front door of the house opened abruptly. Her head jerked up and she stared in astonishment at the woman who stood there.

'Tessa — this is a surprise! Do come in.'
It was Margrit Amundsen.

14

The woman came down the path to meet her, obviously pleased. 'How did you know I was here?' she asked.

'I didn't. This is my half-day, so I took a bus-ride.'

'But why to Vijne, of all places?'

'Why not? I want to see the surrounding country and the bus terminus is here. The man who keeps the post office pointed this house out to me. He said it was once the headquarters of the Freedom Fighters, so I came to see it.'

Margrit smiled and led her into the house.

'That's true. It is Vijne's sole claim to fame, and few even remember that now. Wait a moment while I open the shutters again — another five minutes and you would have missed me, I was just about to leave. Sorry I can't offer you a cup of tea, but the electricity is turned off and china all packed away.'

Tessa looked around, surprised and bewildered. This wasn't the house of a needy widow. She asked hesitantly, 'Do you own it?'

'This house?' Margrit laughed. 'Good gracious, no. I merely keep an eye on it. In other words, I act as caretaker. Come — I'll show you round.'

She took her on a tour of the place, making a running commentary as she went, but Tessa scarcely heeded much of it, catching only occasional references to various rooms and their uses during the war. The place was so well furnished that she found it difficult to associate it with travel-weary men coming and going on clandestine missions while others stayed here at base, glued to secret radios while directing operations. She followed in Margrit's wake with a sense of unreality because none of this was what she expected — least of all to meet Kerstin's mother and be received almost as a guest. Margrit walked from room to room as if she had lived here all her life.

'You know the house well,' Tessa said.

'As indeed I should — I used to spend weeks here with Nina and her parents. It was their holiday home, and when war broke out and things went wrong in Norway her father offered it to the Freedom Fighters — they, of course, had to go back to England quickly, or be interned. After the war Nina's father came back to the British Consulate in Oslo and when her parents died she inherited this place. I keep an eye on it for her.'

'You mean Nina Hyerdal?' Tessa didn't know why she was so surprised.

'Of course. We were at school together. Who told you about her?'

'Carlota.'

'Oh — then that's all right. Carlota has no sympathy for Nina, but she doesn't speak maliciously about her, as others do. I wouldn't have liked you to hear about Nina from anyone else.'

'Does she come here often?'

'Scarcely ever, and then only with friends who have a yacht and can sail straight here. It could be embarrassing both for her and Lars if she landed at Balestrand and then travelled on. People would see her and he'd be sure to hear — as you may have gathered, people are quick to gossip in country places.' She flashed a sympathetic glance. 'Personally, I've no time for that sort of thing. Must you catch that bus back? I could give you a lift. I use one of the company cars when I come here — Max insists upon it. He's a considerate man.'

Tessa let the final remark pass, but took her up on the offer of a lift. The car was parked behind the house in an accessible lane and as they drove away she said, 'It seems a shame that such a lovely place should be unlived in. When did Nina Hyerdal last stay here?'

'In the spring. She brought friends from Oslo — she has a job there now, on a woman's magazine. *Fashion*, it's called, and right up her street. She was trained as a beautician before she married.' Margrit sighed regretfully. 'She has cut herself off from her old life and everyone associated with it, although I believe Max visits her now and then. He bears his mother no malice for deserting his father, which is wonderful of him in the circumstances. One might have expected a son to be biased.' Margrit sighed regretfully. 'Nina doesn't even want to hear from me, one of her oldest friends. A monthly cheque is paid into my bank in return for keeping an eye on things, and I report to her agent if anything needs doing to the house. Otherwise, no contact whatsoever. Poor Nina, I'm afraid she was always rather selfish and spoilt. Not that she can be blamed for that, of course. All the same, I miss her. The bonds of lifelong friendship are strong.'

Tessa scarcely heard a word. Only one fact stood out — that Nina Hyerdal had been here last spring. *Last spring when the anonymous letter had been posted from Vijne.*

170

At last she had definite identification of someone who had actually been on the spot at that time. More than that, it was a person who had every reason to hate James Pickard. Nina Hyerdal would obviously blame him for her husband's accident and, very likely, for wrecking her marriage. From the sound of things she was a woman who enjoyed life, was accustomed to being indulged, fond of gaiety and masculine attention, unable to accept the restrictions imposed upon her by a crippled husband. All this Tessa had gleaned from Carlota's description, and although Margrit didn't condemn her, she did admit that she had always been selfish and spoilt. This was indicative enough, coming from a friend.

The man Nina had married had been the one in the photograph, not the cripple in a wheelchair, and this was good reason for hating the man blamed for the injury. The whole thing was obvious, and so was the woman's character — small-minded, selfish, petty and cruel. That was Nina Hyerdal; a woman capable of mean and unscrupulous behaviour, the very woman to sit down and write tauntingly: '*Do you remember the Jostedal Glacier?*' and leave it unsigned. No signature would be necessary, because what it really said was: '*I haven't forgotten *and I'll never forgive you.'*

Tessa went straight to Carlota when Margrit dropped her at the hotel, and asked if she could have three days' leave. 'I'd like a break, a few days away, and you were saying the other day that a trip would do me good.'

'I was indeed and I meant it. Where do you propose to go?'

'I'd like to see Oslo. I've never been there.'

'Then it's a *must* — but you can't stay in Oslo on your own. You'll need someone to take you around, someone who knows the place and speaks your language as well as Norwegian, although, of course, English is spoken almost universally there. But a girl needs an escort in a city, and I expect you'd enjoy Steve's company.' She smiled knowingly and Tessa smiled back, letting her think she was right. If everyone thought that, no one would ever suspect how she felt about Max.

The following Tuesday she and Steve boarded the Oslo train at Myrdal and Tessa let him imagine that her excitement was due solely to the trip. The true reason she kept to herself. She was going to contact Nina Hyerdal. She was going to meet the writer of the anonymous note. Face to face.

★ ★ ★

It was easy enough to trace the address of *Fashion* through the telephone directory in her hotel room. She went straight there without bothering to unpack, leaving a note at the reception desk for Steve, saying she had gone shopping and would see him later. Then she took a taxi to the magazine offices and asked for Mrs. Hyerdal.

'Have you an appointment, please?'

'No, but I think she'll see me. Tell her it's James Pickard's daughter, from England.'

In revealing her identity Tessa banked on two things, either that Nina would be so taken by surprise that she would be unable to invent a quick excuse, or that curiosity would get the better of her. Curiosity apparently won, for within a matter of minutes the girl returned and asked Tessa to follow her. They walked down a long corridor flanked by doors on either side, amidst a hum of typewriters and ringing telephones and busy voices, then turned off the hive into a shorter passage with a door at the end marked 'Beauty Editor'.

That fitted, according to Carlota's description and Margrit's information. With looks and qualifications no wonder Nina Hyerdal had been able to take off for

173

a new life in Oslo, even in middle age. Beauty could get a woman a long way and it had landed Nina here. Tessa knew what to expect — an immaculate, carefully made-up, well-preserved, handsome woman; a woman belying her years with every form of cosmetic. Blonde? Brunette? Red-head? She could be any colour these days; age was no barrier, with hair tints as natural as they were now and a variety of wigs forming part of many a woman's wardrobe.

Tessa knew what else Nina Hyerdal would be. Superficial. Sophisticated. Brittle. Slim as a reed through careful dieting and hard as the lacquer on her fingernails. Superbly confident too, but she, Tessa Pickard, would deflate her. That was why she had come.

The girl was holding the door open. Tessa braced herself and walked in.

At the far end of the room a woman rose. She was tall — almost as tall as Max, her son. That Tessa had expected, but not the rest of her; not the quiet elegance, the simplicity, the lovely face framed in smooth white hair, the gentle eyes and mouth. Not the unaffected smile and the warm voice and the utter niceness of her. These were the things which made up her beauty and not one was artificial. She left an immediate and indelible impression of being a thoroughly nice woman.

They stood looking at each other for a moment, Nina with interest, Tessa with surprise, and the older woman was the first to speak.

'So you are James's daughter. You are like him.'

She even sounded glad, and looked it. Her welcome was so disarming that Tessa had to steel herself against it. She opened her handbag quickly and took out the anonymous letter, thrusting it out abruptly and demanding 'Why did you send *this* to him?'

15

There was a moment of silence, then Nina Hyerdal stretched out her hand and took the letter, but all the time her eyes never left Tessa's face and the interest that had been in them was subtly replaced by a shadow of bewilderment, because her glance seemed to hold a question, as if she didn't know what Tessa was talking about.

She looked at the envelope and said, 'What has this to do with me?'

'Read it.'

Unwillingly, she took out the note. One glance, and her face went rigid, and for all the world Tessa could have believed it was caused by shock. Then the woman stared for a long moment before saying, 'You think *I* wrote *this*?'

'Look at the postmark. And the date. Vijne, last April, when you were there.'

Nina Hyerdal looked at it as if finding it distasteful, but there seemed to be something else — a flicker in her eyes which Tessa chose to interpret as guilt. Then she said, 'I think you had better sit down, Miss Pickard.'

Tessa was only too willing, for suddenly

she realised she was shaking and that coming here had been a greater ordeal than expected. There was no triumph in her meeting with this woman; none of the elation she had anticipated. She wanted to get the whole thing over and make her escape, because nothing was working out as planned. Even the principal character was different. It would have been easy if Nina Hyerdal had turned out to be the woman she had visualised. In the circumstances Tessa felt almost defrauded.

Nina went back to her desk and sat down. Her movements were composed and graceful, and Tessa recalled Carlota's description of how men gravitated towards her at parties. Now she could well believe it. Max's mother was one of those ageless women whom men would continue to fall in love with throughout the years. A rarity, but that was what she was.

The strange thing was that Tessa couldn't be jealous of this quality in her, as many women might have been, and this inability had nothing to do with the confidence of youth. In other circumstances she would have liked and admired Nina Hyerdal. She would have hoped to resemble her at that age, but Tessa wasn't prepared to acknowledge this yet. Predominantly she felt cheated because the woman had turned out to be the exact opposite of what she expected.

Max's mother said briskly, 'Yes, I was in Vijne last April. I could have posted this letter, had I arrived there on this particular date, but I didn't. I arrived later.'

'I don't believe it.'

Tessa was deliberately on the defensive because she couldn't bear the thought of being wrong. This woman *had* to be the writer. It couldn't be anyone else. Not crippled Lars, bound to his wheelchair in Balestrand. Not Max, because she couldn't bear the thought. Not Kerstin, because if it were, then she couldn't have more positive proof of the girl's intimacy and collaboration with him. Not Thor, because he had no motive, and certainly not Margrit because there was no malice in her — nor did she have a reason. But this woman had reason enough, and a house in Vijne into the bargain. She had been there at the time, whatever she might say.

Tessa refused to look into those calm grey eyes because they now held a pleading which she didn't want to see.

'It *was* you. It must have been you. I've only your word that you arrived later.'

'True,' Nina answered thoughtfully, 'and

obviously you're not prepared to accept my word.'

'Would you, in the circumstances?'

'I don't know what the circumstances are.'

She certainly slung the arrows back adroitly.

Tessa said mutinously, 'You must know. I expect you read about him in the Press. That was how you found out where he was.'

'If you mean your father, I've known where he was for years,' Nina answered calmly.

Tessa was struck dumb.

'And don't say again that you don't believe me, because it's true and if necessary I can prove it. Also if necessary I can prove that I didn't write this — thing.'

She tossed the letter on to her desk as if it were contaminating, and all of a sudden Tessa felt completely out of her depth. Like a frightened and bewildered child, she wanted to cry. It was absurd and infuriating. She took out her handkerchief and blew her nose hard.

'I think some tea would be a good idea, don't you? And do tell me your Christian name. I refuse to call you Miss Pickard.'

'T-Tessa.'

Nina stretched out a hand and pressed the switch of an inter-com, ordered tea for two,

179

and switched off again.

'That's the English in me. I was brought up to have tea at four and can tell the time without even looking at my watch.'

Tessa smiled unwillingly.

'And while we're waiting for it,' Nina continued, 'tell me why you think I wrote that detestable thing?'

'To hurt him, of course. To hit back.'

'My dear child, never in my life did I want to hit back at James. I loved him.'

* * *

The tea arrived almost before Tessa could regain her breath. Nina poured a cup and handed it across. 'Drink that,' she said. 'It will do you good.'

She couldn't have been more right. Tessa hadn't tasted tea like it since she left home.

'And I must say,' Nina went on, 'that feeling the way you do I admire your guts for coming to face me. But you take a lot of convincing, don't you? So I'd better convince you thoroughly and then we can talk.'

She drew a sheet of paper towards her, picked up a pen, and wrote. Then she handed it over, together with the anonymous note. 'Compare them — and you must admit that I wrote spontaneously, so I couldn't

180

disguise my hand. I imagine that would be difficult and laborious.'

The two writings were totally different. Tessa dropped the papers into her lap and stared at the woman in silence.

'And now we *can* talk,' Nina said. 'I'll do the talking and you can do the listening, although I know that isn't the way you wanted it to be.' Her mouth flickered with amusement, then was serious. 'I'd been married to Lars for eight years when James arrived in this country with a unit of British skiers to link up with our own. Lars brought him home one day and I liked him at once. Anyone who met your father couldn't fail to like him, but I never dreamed that I could feel more than that, and I'm not making excuses for myself because I did. These things happen between men and women, and until they do you've no comprehension of how it can feel. I loved my husband and son, but this attraction between James and myself was something completely outside all that, not detracting from it but certainly conflicting. I never realised before that it is possible to love two men, the way a man can love two women, in totally different ways. It took me by surprise, I didn't want it to happen. Neither did James, but human nature can't always command itself. We tried to. James tried and I tried. I tried so hard that I used to pray for him to be posted back home to England and out of my life, because I wanted the problem removed for me. I was twenty-seven and that seemed to me to be an age when I should know how to handle an emotional crisis. As it turned out, I didn't.'

'And Lars guessed?'

'I couldn't hide it. I would never have made my living as an actress. Tell me — how much do you know?'

'That my father is believed to have tried to kill your husband on the Jostedal Glacier.'

'And who told you?'

'Max.'

That hurt her. She was right — she would never have made an actress; her sensitive face revealed personal emotions too easily.

'So you know my son. Where did you meet him?'

Tessa told her.

'Poor Max,' his mother said gently, 'he was a child at the time. He adored his father and Lars was a fine man, a good man. He was a legendary figure even before the accident, a noted skier and mountaineer, and, of course, to Max he was the greatest hero in the world. I wouldn't have spoilt that image for anything. Tarnish a child's ideals and

182

you can hurt him badly. You can destroy his faith and do irreparable harm, and to tell him that I didn't believe his father's story about what happened on the glacier would have stunned the boy. To suggest that his father was a liar — he would have hated me for that. Besides, I didn't think Lars was lying, although I know that sounds contradictory. He was delirious when found and in his delirium snatches of reality came through; his hatred of James because he had come between us; accusations and insults he had apparently hurled at him when they were alone together. And the fight they had — he relived that too. James admitted all this had happened and that finally he was so enraged by the things Lars said that he struck him. They fought. James himself bore physical signs of blows, but swore they had both called a halt and made a pact to complete their mission and settle their differences later.

'And so they went on. It was shortly after that, according to James, that Lars caught one of his skis in a crevasse; it twisted and sprained his ankle. Despite this he kept going, but after a time he urged James to go ahead without him; he was slowing him down and the mission was urgent. *One* of them had to get the message to Vijne.

James said he left Lars protected behind a pinnacle — if you saw the Jostedal you'd know that here and there gigantic spikes rear up like towers. They're called *séracs* and are continually forming with the movement of the glacier. Sometimes they create great barriers and walls — that's when they've fallen due to melting during warm weather. They're best crossed at night, because then, even in summer, the temperature drops to zero and they remain static.'

'And it was summer when they crossed?'

'Yes, but the route was chosen carefully. The glacier was well charted to avoid all but the minimum of movement, which always veers towards a certain point just beyond Fjaerland. You may have seen the overhanging cornice.'

'Yes. It's awe-inspiring. I've heard that it avalanches sometimes, but I've never seen that happen.'

'It avalanches when movement takes place in the glacier above — maybe miles further inland. The original movement might have occurred days before; it's usually slow, and freezes up overnight, then the movement begins again the next day and so it goes on until eventually it reaches that point on the edge of the mountain, and the power behind it bursts the overhang and down it comes.

And that's what I believe happened to Lars. I believe he was carried on an unexpected movement of the ice to the spot where he was found, and that a falling *sérac* injured him fatally.'

'But when he recovered consciousness, didn't he remember?'

'I don't know. I honestly don't know. Anyway, the story he told was entirely different from your father's and never varied. It's my opinion that Lars himself believed it completely, and still does. And the evidence supported him — the spot where he was found, far from that to which James sent the rescue party. His injuries, too. It was his word, plus the evidence, against James's and his lack of it. To make things worse, everyone knew there was jealousy between them. Very real jealousy. And Lars, of course, was the one with right on his side. It was inevitable that James should be blamed.'

'Was that why you stayed with your husband — because he had right on his side, because it was your duty?'

'No. I stayed because I loved him. I loved him deeply and sincerely. I stayed because when it came to a choice I knew that my love for Lars was stronger than the way I felt for James. Unhappily it was too late to convince Lars of that. He believed I stayed with him

185

out of pity, and he clung to that belief for the rest of our life together. Gradually it poisoned our marriage and finally drove me away. I lost all hope of ever making him believe in my love. A man won't accept something unless he wants to, and Lars was no longer the good-natured man he had once been, but withdrawn and embittered and mistrustful. Life was terrible for him, I know.'

Tessa said gently, 'It must have been terrible for you too.'

'It wasn't — easy. In the end I knew I was doing no good by staying. I couldn't help him. Even the sight of me seemed to aggravate his mistrust and stir up all the old memories. And he used to have nightmares — one recurring nightmare which he would never reveal. He used to blame me for it. I thought that if I went away, the nightmares might cease. I was a constant reminder, a constant reproach to a man who had lost the power to forgive.'

'And — Max?'

'Max was old enough to see how things were between us and to feel for both of us. My son and I are not estranged. When he can, he comes to Oslo to visit me. He never asks questions about the past and I never refer to it, but I know he believes his father's story about what happened on the glacier.'

'And hates *my* father because of it.'

Nina sighed. 'Yes, I'm afraid he does. He has grown up with that as a legacy and Lars's condition never lets him forget it. Max still thinks the world of his father, and I'm glad of that, but I have never believed James guilty and I never will. He wasn't the type of man to leave another to die, no matter what jealousy existed between them, nor how bitterly they had quarrelled and fought. Such an action just wasn't in character.'

'Thank you,' Tessa said quietly. 'Thank you.' The words sounded inadequate, but conveyed a lot.

'As for this . . . ' Nina indicated the anonymous note, 'how did you come by it? Surely James didn't give it to you? He would have torn up a thing like that.'

'But he didn't. He kept it. I found it amongst his things when I went through them.'

Nina said with a catch in her breath, 'Amongst — his things?'

So she didn't know. Tessa told her everything, from the time of the Wynyard affair to his death, and how it had happened. She sat for a long time, very still, very white, and for the first time since Tessa had walked into this room she looked old.

At last she whispered, 'Poor James — was there no justice for him in this life?'

Tessa couldn't answer because she wanted to cry out that that was why she was here, and why she intended to remain, and why she would keep on and on until she achieved justice for him.

'I hope he married happily,' Nina said. 'I've never forgotten him, nor the feeling there was between us, even though it wasn't meant to last. Having you must have meant a great deal to him. He knew how much my own child meant to me.'

'We were close — very close, I think.'

She didn't ask about James's wife and Tessa was glad, for now she understood that rushed marriage. Its motivation had been forgetfulness, need, sex. And right at that moment something else struck her — a possible reason for Ruth's attraction and his inability to take his eyes off her when first they met. Ruth had been tall and graceful, like this woman. She had been blonde, as Nina must have been, but unlike Nina she had carefully remained so. The two women had certain features in common — a short straight nose, grey eyes, pointed chin, wide brow. But there the similarity ended. Nina Hyerdal had enough character to face up to problems and to endure them for years.

Ruth ran away from them. And if James had married her on the rebound Tessa was quite sure her mother had never suspected it — nor, perhaps, had he. She was also sure that he had married Ruth genuinely believing he had fallen in love again. Perhaps he had, for a while, but when work became the big consolation in his life it wasn't because Ruth was a bad wife but because she was the wrong one for him and he the wrong husband for her.

Nina's voice recalled her.

'So on the strength of that cruel note and its revealing postmark you took a chance and came to Norway to track down the writer?'

'Of course.'

'You *are* like your father. You have his courage and determination. But what hope have you of succeeding?'

'Well, the outlook's blank, I admit. You were my prime suspect and I haven't another. But I won't give up. I'll find the person who wrote this. I'll defend James if it's the last thing I do. There must be *some* justice for him eventually.'

Nina looked at her with compassion, but Tessa didn't want it. She wanted help.

'When you first saw this letter,' she said, 'something struck you. What was it?'

'Disgust.'

'I thought I saw something else — a flicker, a thought, a question perhaps. I don't know what it was, but I saw *some*thing.'

'Shock, naturally.'

'Not recognition? The writing wasn't familiar to you?'

For a moment Nina Hyerdal seemed to hesitate, then the sharp ring of a telephone cut into the moment and she switched her attention to it. Tessa heard a male voice at the end of the line saying something about a doublespread, and Nina replying, 'No — don't bother to bring them along. I'll come to you.'

Replacing the receiver she asked Tessa to excuse her while she went along to the art department to look at some layouts. 'A special beauty supplement and they want my approval. Don't go away — I'll be back as soon as I can. Help yourself to cigarettes.'

She smiled warmly and departed. Not until Tessa reached for a cigarette from her desk did she realise that Nina had taken the anonymous letter and its envelope.

She felt a dart of apprehension. Was the woman a superb actress, after all? Was she to be trusted? Why should she remove the letter, and what if she failed to return with it? After the first shock Tessa felt stung to action, but forced herself to be calm. After all, she knew where to trace her — the art department. If Nina Hyerdal didn't come back within ten minutes she would hunt her down; announce that she had to leave, and ask outright for the letter. The woman would be unlikely to face a dispute in front of the office staff, although Tessa was perfectly willing to have one if necessary. She was resolved not to leave this building without that letter.

She didn't have to. Nina returned quite soon with some papers in her hand, and an apology. 'I took this by mistake,' she said as she put the papers in a drawer. 'Forgive me. I imagine you don't want to lose it, objectionable as it is. It's your only weapon, isn't it?'

She handed the letter over. Tessa accepted it, weak with relief, and automatically glanced inside the envelope to check the contents. The note was there, quite untampered with. She thrust it in her handbag, embarrassed and slightly ashamed, convinced that Nina Hyerdal knew of her sudden doubt and suspicion, but the woman's smile was still kind, still understanding.

'You're right,' Tessa answered ruefully. 'It is my only weapon — and it still hasn't got me anywhere.'

★ ★ ★

191

Steve looked at her and said, 'Well, that was one helluva shopping spree from the look of things.'

She was completely empty-handed.

'I couldn't find a *thing* I wanted!' She feigned exhaustion. 'Hoofing round the Oslo shops is as bad as hoofing around London.'

'In that case you could do with a drink.'

'Give me five minutes — no, ten — and I'll meet you in the bar.'

She changed in record time, pulling an uncrushable dress out of her unpacked bag. She hadn't brought much — the things she had travelled in, overnight gear, and this one simple frock. Two minutes to remove her make-up, five to replace it, a few more to brush her hair until it shone and her scalp tingled, then a couple more to step into her dress, zip it up, slip on her shoes, cast a comprehensive and critical glance in the mirror, pick up her handbag and head for the lift.

'Three minutes behind schedule,' Steve said. 'I'll forgive you for that, but not for this afternoon's desertion. Now isn't that like a woman, to go haring off to the shops without giving a thought to a mere male kicking his heels waiting for her?'

'I'll bet the mere male didn't wait long,' she chaffed, and picked up the Campari-soda he had lined up for her. 'This is good — I needed it. Bless you, Steve.'

'I want more than a bless you, but this isn't the time or place.'

She dodged that. 'What did you do during heel-kicking time?'

'Went for a walk up Karl Johans Gate — the whole length, right up to the Palace. I thought I might bump into you around the shops, but no luck. Where on earth did you get to?'

Mercifully, a waiter approached with a couple of outsize menus, asking if *Min Herre* would care to order, and they turned their attention to dinner. The bar was a pleasant one and after the man had bowed himself away they sat back and relaxed. By the time the waiter returned to announce that their table was ready, Tessa had downed another Campari and discovered that she was ravenously hungry.

She also discovered something else — Steve hadn't been joking when he said that he wanted more than a bless you. His hand found hers beneath the table more than once, and for a while she wondered if she was in for a problem trip after all.

Reading her thoughts, he said, 'I want it if you do, but not if you don't, and you know what I'm talking about. I won't force myself on you, if that's what you're afraid of, but you must know I love you. Everybody else has guessed, and Carlota must think you reciprocate since you jumped at her suggestion that I should come along to keep an eye on you.'

'Day and night?'

'If I have my way.'

'That wasn't her idea at all.'

'I didn't imagine so. Carlota thinks I'm the clean and honourable type with whom any mother could trust her virgin daughter.'

'And aren't you?'

'I know how to behave myself when necessary. I just hoped it wouldn't be, that's all. I'm mad about you, but whatever way you want it, that's the way it will be.'

'I'll tell you how I want it. I enjoy your company. Let's keep it like that, shall we? Intimacy often means the end of things.'

'So you're not in love with me?'

'I'm not in love with any man,' she lied.

'That I don't believe. When a woman's in love there's something about her, a kind of awareness, a kind of life.'

'Even when she's unhappily in love?'

'Even then. She's *feeling* something. And you're doing that all right, honey, even if it isn't for me. I take it it's someone back home?'

194

She let him draw his own conclusions by remaining silent, and later, when they danced, he held her very close and she liked it. She liked it because she was unhappy and lonely and in need of comfort, but these were the wrong reasons for accepting a man's love.

'Let's be together tonight,' he begged. 'Forget whoever it is and let yourself go, for God's sake.'

'I thought you only wanted it if I did.'

'I'll make you want it, my lovely. Before this evening is over, I'll make you.'

'No, Steve. I didn't come to Norway to forget anyone, or to find a lover, or to have an affair. I could do that at home.'

'Now that's where you're wrong — you wouldn't have met *me* there, so aren't you glad you came after all?'

His good nature was irrepressible and she blessed him for it, and for being so even-tempered and uncomplicated. She even wished she could love him. She wished the fondness she felt for him could develop into something deeper and drive out all thought of Max with his unpredictable swings of mood and passionate prejudices and dark personality, but now that she had met his mother she found herself thinking of the child who had adored his father and had seen him change from a strong, vital man into a physical wreck whose sole consolation in life was painting the mountains he could no longer climb, and the snow-fields and glaciers he could no longer ski across.

That child had grown up to see his parents' marriage disintegrate through doubt on one side and despair on the other, and all because of what had happened on the frozen ceiling of the mountains, due to one man, years ago. In his father's eyes that man had been responsible for everything and so, inevitably, in the boy's eyes too. In the circumstances it wasn't surprising that Max had grown into the kind of man he was, and this was the man she had fallen in love with.

Why couldn't one fall in love to order, she thought wretchedly as Steve's lips brushed her cheek. When she didn't turn away his hold tightened and a warm feeling of gratitude filled her, making her brush his lips lightly in return. She felt no sexual reaction to the contact, and he knew it. He stopped dancing and led her back to their table, and they finished the meal in silence. When it was over he said, 'Time to pack the evening up, unless you want a brandy?'

She didn't. They went up in the lift together and he said good night at her door. When she started to speak he burst out, 'Don't say you're sorry, for God's sake. You either feel it, or you don't. You either want it, or you don't.' A poor imitation of his normal smile flickered momentarily. 'Sleep well, honey. No hard feelings. But there's nothing I wouldn't do for you, remember that.'

She did remember it later. Much later, after they had returned to Fjaerland and the trip was over. It turned out to be an enjoyable trip after all, with Steve planning every moment of it. They visited the Kon-Tiki raft and the Viking ships at Bygdoy; they went aboard Amundsen's polar expedition ship, handling the helm and touching the things the great explorer had touched, treading the planks he had walked on. They sailed across the Oslo Fjord and lunched at the famous yacht club, of which Steve was a member. After that, the renowned city hall with its modern décor and student guides, then on to Vigeland Park to see the massive outdoor sculptures, immense and apparently never-ending.

'Imagine it,' said Steve. 'One man chiselling his lifetime away to fill a national park!'

'That's dedication for you.'

'Overdone, I think. There's just too much of it and all overpowering — except the children's corner. Let's drive out to Holmenkollen — *that* will awe you if you've never seen a championship ski-jump.'

They went up in the lift to the towering peak which was the start of the ski-run, and the whole of Oslo and its wide fjord could be seen spread out like a patterned carpet far below, then they descended to the restaurant over which the skiers leapt *en route*, still hundreds of feet up. The thought of these incredible athletes skimming over the roof like gigantic snow birds left her breathless.

It was quite a day. By the time they had wound it up with a visit to the National Theatre and supper in a night club they were both too tired to do anything but say good night. No talk of love, no overtures, no complications, and only time for a shopping spree in the morning.

Steve looked at her stack of parcels and said wryly, 'No difficulty in finding what you wanted today, my lovely?' and all she could do was laugh. Then they were rushing for the train back to Myrdal, and Olaf waiting with the hotel launch at Flaam, at the foot of the spiral mountain railway.

The trip was over. Only then did she realise that in bringing her nearer to the anonymous letter-writer it had availed her absolutely nothing, but in bringing her nearer to the truth about her father's past it had been a gigantic step forward. She was glad she had met Nina Hyerdal and felt that the meeting had been important.

But had the woman really taken that anonymous letter by accident? In view of her initial reluctance to touch it, Tessa couldn't believe anything else.

16

It was the following night, after she had finished for the day, that she heard someone outside her cabin. She had dined in the hotel and returned late; showered, prepared for bed, then tied a thin wrap over her nightdress and sat down before the quaint Norwegian stove to browse over her shopping. She had dropped into bed without unpacking a thing when reaching home last night, and had been on duty at the reception desk at eight-thirty this morning, so her parcels were still unopened. Now she untied them leisurely, scattering paper and string, enjoying her extravagance and refusing to tot up what she had spent. She hadn't indulged in such a shopping spree for a long time.

She was trying out a new hand cream when she first heard the sound — a footstep on gravel, then another, and another. A man's tread, coming straight to her door. She thought with faint annoyance that it must be Steve, refusing to take no for an answer. She was disappointed and hoped he wasn't going to spoil their friendship by pushing it.

The footsteps mounted her porch. The door wasn't locked. She had fallen into the habit of other staff members who kept their doors on the latch, popping into each other's cabins for a smoke or a chat or to borrow things. Locks were only dropped at night, or when out. She called, 'If it's someone wanting to borrow something, come in and help yourself.'

She fully expected it to be Steve and was ready to despatch him firmly should he have other ideas, but as the latch lifted she knew she was wrong. She was familiar with his casual way of flicking up the latch with his forefinger and letting it drop as the door swung open. This time the touch was different; stronger and more deliberate.

It was Max.

She stared, too astonished to say a word. He stood framed in the doorway, his hand still on the latch, then said easily, 'My apologies — you're in a draught,' and closed the door behind him. Without giving her an opportunity to speak he continued, 'I came to ask a question which I've been wanting to ask for some time. When we met at the folk festival you were saying something about an anonymous letter when Hatton interrupted. He did so again on the quay at Balestrand. I've been away, or I would have come before.

I want to see that letter.'

'I can believe that, but neither you nor Kerstin are going to get your hands on it.'

'Kerstin? What has she to do with it?'

'As much as you, I imagine. Did she search this place on your behalf to get it back, or did she write it for you? A woman will do anything for a man she's going to marry, and I understand you two are.'

'It's possible,' he admitted carelessly, 'but I didn't come here to discuss my marriage plans. I came about a letter which, you said, had driven your father to take his life, sent anonymously from here.'

'*Near* here. But I've said all I want to say.'

'And I haven't.'

'You said enough the day we went climbing, and all of it lies.'

'As *this* was?' He took hold of her roughly and his kiss was passionate and unrestrained. There was nothing gentle about it, nor about the way he held her, hard and unyielding. She was aware of his overriding demand and desire, and although she wanted to break free, she couldn't. His mouth held hers until she was passive and responsive. She could feel the pressure of his hands through her nightdress, and back came the hot desire she had experienced that first time, but deeper and more passionate so that control began to ebb.

He burst out, 'I can't get you out of my mind and I can't keep away from you, damn you. I wish to God you'd get out of my life.'

She gasped, 'You're doing everything you can to persuade me to stay in it!

'I want you, that's why.'

'But you don't love me, nor I you.' With sudden resolution she broke free and stood with her arms crossed about her shaking body, facing him. 'You want to strike back, don't you? Against my father and, because of him, against me. You're ruthless and bigoted and cruel. It would give you satisfaction to have your way with me now as you have with other women; to use me as you've used them and discard me afterwards, because that's the kind of man you are. You'd like to humiliate James Pickard's daughter just because she *is* James Pickard's daughter and the man himself has gone beyond your reach. *You* sent him there, stabbing him after all these years!'

He blazed, 'I don't know what the hell you're talking about. I know nothing about any anonymous letter. *That* is why I'm here.'

'But your mother knows about it. I've

shown it to her. I went to Oslo and talked with her, and I'll tell you something — she knows who wrote it. I'm certain of that. She recognised the writing and kept silent. Why, I wonder — because it was yours, or your embittered father's, and she wouldn't betray either of you?' Tessa was shaking with rage and when he opened his mouth in swift protest she rushed on: 'And I'll tell you something else. Your mother isn't cruel and vindictive like you, and I don't blame her for running away from her self-pitying husband!'

His hand whipped out and stung her cheek. It was like the crack of a whip, cutting off her words. They stood staring at each other, too shaken to speak, and she could feel the blood rushing to her smarting cheek, outlining the weal he had left. He looked at it, appalled, then without a word he strode out of the place. The door crashed behind him.

17

Someone leaned across the reception desk and said, 'You look as if you've had a bad night. Didn't you sleep?'

It was Steve, his handsome, wholesome face smiling at her.

'No,' she said. 'I was over-tired. All that travelling . . . '

'What you need is fresh air. There's no wind for sailing, but I'll come with you on one of those long walks of yours. How about it? As soon as you're off duty?'

'That'll be fine. I check off at five.'

He was ready and waiting, and she turned automatically towards the village. Steve fell into step beside her and she was grateful for his inconsequential chatter. It was true that she hadn't slept. She had lain the whole night through too shaken by her experience with Max, reliving every moment of that wild, passionate, and disturbing scene. She had wept too, bitterly and for a long time.

In the morning the mark of his blow still showed on her cheek, so that she had to disguise it with make-up. Now it had subsided, and fresh air and exercise did the rest, whipping a glow to her face and unconsciously lifting her spirits. She would never see him again. He would never come near her again — she was certain of that, and was thankful. Falling in love with a man like Max Hyerdal was something she wanted to recover from as quickly as possible.

'You take this walk a lot,' Steve said as the village receded. 'I've often seen you head this way. Why?'

'I like to see the glacier. It fascinates me.'

'Is that where we're going now?'

'Yes. Do you mind?'

'Not if you're set on it, but I must admit I find that particular spot a bit chilling, to put it mildly. In fact, it's damned eerie, but mountains don't appeal to me, as you know.'

'And you can't feel the fascination of that overhanging ice?'

'Not a bit. Too damn menacing.'

When they arrived at the spot it seemed quite a time since she had been there. She looked up at the projecting shelf and said, 'It seems to have grown. I'm sure it's bigger than the last time I came.' On an impulse she took Steve's hand and pulled him towards the ice tunnel. 'I've never been inside — come with me.'

'No, thanks. I once ventured a few yards and that was enough. It's perishing cold and wet in there and I shouldn't sample it in those clothes, if I were you.

She brushed that aside, telling him to wait if that was the way he felt, and stepped carefully over the wet shingle which edged the fjord. The frozen hill was unique and interesting, ice-hard roof and exterior walls sparkling like diamonds. The entrance to the tunnel was arched and penetrated deeply into its centre, with the hard outer casing rigid and unyielding. It had stood here for years, constantly being fortified by further deposits of ice from above, but, as Steve said, the interior wasn't too pleasant and she soon turned back.

'You were right,' she called. 'Next time I'll wear water-proofs!'

She pushed the damp hair back from her face and splashed across the wet shingle to join him. He was sitting on a rock with his back towards the mountainside. The fjord interested him more.

'The fishing here is good,' he said. 'If it weren't for that damned glacier I'd come more often.'

'Do you really think it's dangerous?' She sat down beside him and gazed up at the towering rock-face. They were a few hundred yards away from the glacier point, near the safe traverse which she had mapped on her climbing route.

'Of course it's dangerous.' Steve handed her a cigarette and she drew on it with enjoyment, watching the smoke curl upwards in the clear air. 'Don't take solitary walks here any more. Promise?'

'You must be joking.'

'I'm dead serious. Heed what I tell you, that's all.'

'Well, now I'll tell *you* something — if one started over there to the right, one could climb this mountain face in safety and reach the top in two or three days. Imagine it! Imagine standing up there and looking out across the frozen ceiling of the world!'

'You must be crazy, girl.'

'I'm not. I want to do it. It isn't an ideal solo climb, so how about coming with me? Let's tackle it together.'

'Not on your life!'

'You'd said you'd do anything for me,' she reminded him.

'Except commit suicide,' he said tactlessly, apparently unaware of the painful reminder. 'You must be out of your mind even to contemplate it. What do you want to do — torture yourself by looking at the scene where your father left a man to die?'

She blazed back: 'He did no such thing, and you know it. You said yourself that never in a million years would James Pickard be capable of murder!'

'I had to say something to reassure you, honey. You were in a state at the time, remember. But do we ever really know what a person is capable of? The worst criminals have often looked disarmingly innocent, or so I've heard. As for your father, of course I don't believe him capable of *calculated* murder, but I must admit he wasn't one of my favourite people — unlike his daughter.'

He tried to take her hand, but she pulled away angrily.

'You didn't even know him! You met him once, only once, and then for no more than a minute. Do you bear him a grudge just because he refused to give you an interview?

'What interview?' he asked without thinking.

Tessa crushed out her cigarette slowly. Equally slowly she said, 'You told me you tried to get an interview with my father for that sports journal you worked on. You said he refused it. You said he asked you to excuse him, and off he went — and off you went too, back to your office. You said that was the only time you met him. Briefly.'

Steve's eyes faltered and looked away.

'Well, of course, that's true.'

'I don't believe you. You're lying now and you were lying then.'

He jumped to his feet. 'Come on, let's go. This place doesn't appeal to me.'

'I won't go until you've answered my question. Did you or did you not meet my father?'

'All right,' he said, as if coming to a decision, 'you can have it. I did more than meet him — I enrolled as a pupil at that climbing school of his, and he had the nerve to tell me at the end of the first term that I'd never make a climber. He told me to quit and stick to what I was good at. The nerve of it!'

All the good nature had disappeared from his face. She stared in disbelief.

'So that story about going to interview him . . . ?'

He shrugged. 'Not true. Does it matter Tess? I wanted to spare your feelings. You mean a lot to me, you know.'

She answered stonily, 'Spare my feelings in what way?'

He said defensively, impatiently, 'I didn't want you to know how I felt about him. I knew it would upset you. You should thank me for being so considerate. *He* didn't spare *my* feelings when he told me I was a failure, and I can well understand that chap Wynyard going out in defiance of him.'

Tessa went numb.

'So — you've known all along . . . '

'About the Wynyard business? Of course. I get newspapers from home. I must admit my sympathy was all with Wynyard and to tell you the truth, honey, I wasn't a bit sorry the school closed down. I think your father got what was coming to him.'

She turned and walked away as fast as she could. Steve had the good sense to let her go.

* * *

She felt as if the last prop had been kicked from under her. Of all people, Steve was the last she would have suspected of duplicity. She had trusted him absolutely, believed every word he said, thought it totally impossible for him to have any motive for disliking her father, and now discovered he had been nursing a grudge against him for a long time. If there was one thing Steve couldn't take, it was failure as a sportsman.

And now, of course, she knew the reason for his dislike of climbing. It wasn't because he had been badly taught, but because he lacked the talent for it, and his vanity was such that it resented being told so. He couldn't be content with excelling in other spheres; he wanted to be the complete all-rounder, hogging the limelight all the way. He was an egoist who couldn't stand having his ego pricked.

Just how deeply could he nurse such a grudge? she wondered as she hurried home. Deeply enough to hide it beneath a gay, inconsequential façade and bide his time until he could hit back? She had imagined there could be no possible reason for Steve to write an anonymous note, besides being incapable of it. She hadn't even considered him as a potential suspect, but now she wasn't so sure. He had known about Wynyard, and the enquiry, and the closing of the school. All this had pleased him. If he was capable of feeling that way, he was capable of adding his own retaliating blow at a moment when it would hurt most.

He knew the Hyerdal story too. It was he who had told her about it, denying that he knew the identity of the Englishman involved. There he had lied again, and since he was capable of so much deception he could have been capable of writing that taunting note, omitting his name because James would probably have remembered it. Perhaps he even experienced greater satisfaction from hitting back silently.

And it would have been easy for him to post the letter from Vijne, to avoid the Fjaerland postmark.

★ ★ ★

She was back in the maze again, suspecting everyone and trusting no one, because whenever she did they let her down. She mentally ticked them off one by one, all those people who bore her father a grudge of some sort. Lars because he was the victim. Max, because he was his son. Kerstin, because she was in love with Max. And now Steve, because James Pickard had wounded his ego. Nina? No, she couldn't believe it of Nina. The woman had seemed too sincere.

But so had Steve.

It was inevitable now that she should withdraw from him. When they came face to face the next day he said, 'Tessa — please. Can't we at least be friends?' and all the old charm was there, the disarming frankness.

'I thought we were,' she answered indifferently, and went on her way. A small deception she could forgive, but to her Steve's was a big one. Max had been cruel, but at least he had been honest. From the moment he learned of her identity, he had

213

shown his colours, and even the other night he had not pretended. He hadn't denied the fact that he desired her only physically. He had wooed her neither with lies, nor words of love.

18

There was now only one thing which occupied her mind — the mountain where her father had made his descent on that fateful day. The foothill became her refuge; she visited it more and more until finally convinced that the route of ascent which she had planned must be the very route he had taken. If she climbed it, she would be treading in his footsteps, but in reverse.

She knew now what she was going to do. She had known all along that she wanted to, and now resolution crystallised. Two weeks later the permanent hotel receptionist returned and time was her own again; the weather was ideal and she had everything in readiness. She decided to tackle the first part of the traverse to test her navigation route; with luck she would reach the halfway mark, after which she would descend, familiarising herself with the terrain in preparation for the summit climb.

She set out early, long before the hotel was astir. No one saw her go. The village was deserted as she walked through. In another hour it would slowly come to life, but right now everyone in the world, except herself, was asleep. The sun came up as she approached the area of the ice tunnel, and when she reached the rock where she had sat with Steve she put on her spiked boots and began to climb, taking it unhurriedly, as she had been taught. The going was laborious, and after a couple of hours she had scaled a far shorter distance than anticipated.

It was then she realised that somewhere, somehow, she had gone wrong. The ridge she was following veered further to the left than she had calculated and had led her towards the area below the glacier shelf. To avoid it meant going back, tackling a vertical groove, and passing a rope through several running belays. For that she needed a partner. Climbing solo demanded auto-protection technique., using a loop of rope clipped to pitons, ascending and descending in turn to clip and unclip the rope.

This was something she had not expected and in which she had no experience. Outstanding climbers in the Alps undertook long and arduous solo expeditions this way, but she would have to practise the technique before tackling the climb again, doing a little more each day until she was thoroughly confident.

With resignation she began the descent,

choosing a shorter route which would land her not far from the ice tunnel and save a lot of time. It proved to be an easy drop, her spikes biting into the rock so that she descended in safety.

She had almost reached the bottom when she heard giant pistol shots reverberating through the skies; mighty cracks of sound, as if the roof of the world was splitting open. She looked up, startled, but the overhanging shelf of the glacier seemed as solid and immovable as ever.

A moment later there was a sudden roar and a gigantic fountain of sparkling ice exploded against the heavens, pelting down the mountainside in shattered fragments.

Tessa jumped. There was a steep drop below and she took it in one leap. She could hear the avalanche increasing, and one petrified glance over her shoulder revealed that it was roaring down towards the valley, a torrent of ice blocks in ever-increasing size. She hurled her cumbrous haversack away, then went scrambling down the sharp pitch, slithering on stones, frantically racing against time and the gathering momentum of sound. Echoes reverberated again and again as ice ricocheted from rock to rock, solid lumps which could injure with one blow.

She had finally reached the ground when

she was struck. Pain seared her shoulder, then a blow on her leg made it buckle under. The cascade became a thunderous torrent and sent her in panic-stricken haste, dragging her injured leg, towards the only shelter strong enough to withstand the onslaught — the tunnel with its roof and walls of solid ice, hard and unyielding as a mountain crag. Urgency gave her unsuspected strength as the path of the avalanche roared nearer. She felt a glancing blow on the back of her neck as an ice-chip as big as an axe-head skimmed off it, but in the near distance was the yawning mouth of the tunnel and her frantic determination was focused upon it.

Suddenly it was there, in front of her. Dazed with pain and shock she crawled inside, as deep inside as she could drag herself, and as she collapsed on the freezing ground she knew that she had crawled into an icy grave where no one would ever find her.

19

The heart of the snow tunnel seemed like the dark centre of the earth, with a distant glimmer of light from the entrance indicating that there was a world outside. For a long time Tessa lay half stunned, aware only of pain mingled with fear, then gradually a feeling of intense cold spread over her, chill as an icy blanket, and through her diminishing senses she could hear the muffled thunder of the avalanche roaring down the mountainside and pounding upon the roof of the tunnel. In a stunned corner of her mind she wondered if it would wall up her retreat and if she would eventually be discovered in deep refrigeration, like bodies frozen by fiction scientists to be thawed back to life at some future date.

Mrs. Rip Van Winkle, that's me, she thought with a desperate clutch at humour, but I'd prefer a twenty-year sleep to being kept indeterminately on ice. Some glimmer of lucidity within her tried to laugh because the idea was meant to be funny, but her lips wouldn't move because, like the rest of her body, they were rapidly stiffening.

Instinct urged her not to close her

eyes because if she did she would lose consciousness completely. She would hear nothing and see nothing. She would have no idea when the avalanche ceased, or when darkness fell, or when footsteps eventually approached — if they ever did. *Shout, call out, don't let your throat freeze up, breathe deeply and keep on shouting . . .* The advice communicated itself, but was futile. All that emerged was a dry croak, a meaningless murmur of sound that came back at her like an echo from the frozen walls of her cave.

Lingering traces of common sense argued that something wasn't quite right about that, but she was too stupefied to work it out until a cold splash on her forehead, followed by another and yet another, hammered the reason home. Her cave wasn't completely frozen if it dripped like this; frozen solid outside, like an Eskimo's igloo, but not within. She tried to grope about her, but found that she could only use one arm because pain from the other shoulder was acute. Nevertheless she touched the stream in which she was half lying, half sitting, and remembered the constant thaw within the tunnel which channelled down to the fjord.

But if she couldn't actually freeze to death, she could certainly die of exposure. She wondered which method would be the quickest, and that same instinct which urged her to fight unconsciousness now forced her to think back to her first-aid training, part of every climber's essential knowledge.

'Treatment for exposure — provide warmth by wrapping the patient in blankets and on no account administer spirits. Brandy or any form of spirit is dangerous for exposure victims. Strong tea with plenty of sugar; hot food for sustenance; never move the victim until rescue team with medical aid arrives . . . ' That feeble croak which was meant to be a laugh forced its way through again. She had thrown away her essential means of survival. Somewhere out there, beneath the avalanche, lay her rucksack with a flask of hot tea, and another of soup, and a sealed cellophane pack of sustaining protein food, and a thick, warm, waterproof sleeping bag which zipped right up to the chin and provided a snug hood for the head and a shield for the face. Everything that was necessary for bivouacking in cold, wet conditions was in that rucksack. It had been her lifeline and she had hurled it away.

But if she had not, she would have been buried beneath ice by now. In the dark shadows of diminishing consciousness she wondered if that might not have been preferable to a slow, relentless death.

Time became meaningless; she had no sensation of its passing. Her eyelids were heavy and becoming heavier, and so was her body. The intense cold penetrated even through her well-designed climbing kit. James had always emphasised that too many accidents happened to climbers because they were ill-equipped or incorrectly shod, but in an emergency such as this not even the best climbing gear was one hundred per cent protective. The most it could do was to postpone the effects of exposure depending upon the duration.

The duration . . . How long would it last, how long would she be able to keep even partially alert, how long before the rumbling mountain became silent, how long before somebody came?

If they came.

She kept her rigid gaze fixed upon the opening of the tunnel. She was half-propped against the ice-cold wall, half-lying upon the ice-cold ground, but gradually a terrifying realisation got through to her — the realisation that all feeling was slipping away, that she was no longer aware of the wetness beneath her body or the dripping water upon her head; that she had reached the point of being impervious to all outer sensation and that even pain was becoming anaesthetised by coldness. She tried to lift a hand, but the fingers were rigid and lifeless so she had no idea whether they moved or not. And the light was going from the tunnel entrance, becoming darker . . . and darker . . . disappearing altogether . . .

That must have been when unconsciousness first took over, because later, much later, some vague awareness saw the distant light again, but dimly, and some mental radar told her that the mountain was quiet. But it didn't matter, none of it mattered, and she welcomed returning darkness because it meant oblivion and absence of all feeling; the end of sensation and pain and coldness and fear. She slipped back into a world of unreality, wanting to remain there because it spread blissfully into eternity. She resented being pulled out of it; she resented being called back; she resented something stronger than herself which was hell-bent on drawing her out of her escape world into one where pain and terror predominated.

Something hot and sweet was seeping into her throat and surging through her veins, and although it was good she resisted, seeking oblivion again, until once more she was drawn out of it, and far away in some remote distance a voice said, 'She's opening her eyes, thank God. She's coming round . . . '

223

But she didn't want to come round. Instinct made her grope once more for that merciful unconsciousness, but this time it was elusive. Her heavy eyelids opened against their will, revealing a man's face looking down into hers, but his features failed to focus properly because his back was towards a dazzling light, a light so strong that it pierced through her eyes into her brain where some half-forgotten knowledge told her that it was a portable quartz-iodine searchlight. It was then that she remembered where she was, and what had happened, and realised that after all she was not dead however much she wanted to be.

The man said, 'Lower that light — it's blinding her. Focus it here, on her leg,' then added something about a Thomas splint, and after that Tessa didn't hear any more because pain sent her pelting back into oblivion. For how long she had no idea, but it seemed no time at all before reality finally took over and she heard the crunching sound of footsteps, was conscious of movement, and saw, in the distance far above, the night sky where stars looked down. She was no longer in the tunnel, but in the open air.

She was being carried on a stretcher and the same man's voice was commanding the rescue party. He was close beside her and his hands guided the stretcher so that no unnecessary jolting caused additional pain. With an effort she turned her head and looked up at him, and saw his lean, hewn features etched in moonlight. He glanced down, and for a second she could have sworn that his expression was one of tenderness and compassion.

Except, of course, that she knew better, because the man was Max and he could never feel that way about her.

20

The room was unfamiliar; spacious and lovely, with a feeling of security and peace. As she emerged from sleep, memories came back one by one — of a woman in a nurse's uniform carefully cutting one leg of her climbing trousers from ankle to thigh; of lying upon an examination couch in a clinical room while a doctor stooped over her. She remembered her arm being sterilised for an injection — after that, nothing.

But later still? Vague loose ends, like Margrit smiling down at her as she held a feeding cup to her lips, and the feeling of blessed comfort and warmth which was with her now. She sank back into it gratefully, but this time kept her eyes open and took a good look round.

A door opened and Margrit entered.

'So you're awake,' she said.

'Wide awake, and trying to work out where I am and how long I've been here.'

'Two days, and you've slept all the time except when I fed you. Even then you scarcely heeded things.'

'You've been nursing me?'

'Of course.'

Tessa looked across at a wide window commanding a magnificent view of water and mountains.

'No wonder you said your flat had a better view than your office.'

Margrit laughed. 'My dear Tessa, you're always mistaking other people's homes for mine. Did you really imagine I could afford anything like this?'

'Then who owns it?

'Lars, of course.'

'Lars Hyerdal! *His* house?'

'Max brought you here. The hospital diagnosed a straightforward fracture of the tibia and a dislocated shoulder. Apart from those injuries there were no complications other than shock and exposure, but unfortunately our small hospital hadn't a spare bed, so after they'd attended to you Max had you brought here by ambulance, then sent for me.'

'Couldn't I have gone back to Fjaerland?'

'That would have been unwise. The village has no doctor and has to rely on our local one, so it was better to keep you in the vicinity. Don't imagine you can leave that bed yet, even if you *are* well enough to sit up and take notice, and don't try to put your right leg to the floor — it's in plaster and will be for some time. You'll need crutches to get around.'

Tessa lay back and moaned.

'How awful! How absolutely *awful* to land up here! Can't I really be moved? Be an angel, Margrit, and fix it. I'm sure I'll be O.K. back in my cabin. The hotel staff will look after me, and with crutches I'll be mobile.'

Margrit smiled sympathetically, but shook her head. 'Out of the question, my dear. Dr. Vansted visits you daily and it wouldn't be fair to expect him to drive out to Fjaerland, now would it? He's a busy man. As for it being awful to land up here, aren't you a little ungrateful? You couldn't recuperate in a more ideal place.'

Tessa hastened to assure her that she appreciated everything, and her nursing in particular.

'You're just about the kindest person I've met since coming here, Margrit, and certainly one of the friendliest.'

The woman looked pleased. 'My dear, I *like* you. I've liked you from the start and what trouble is it to look after someone you like? You'd do the same for me, I'm sure. Now — how about a cup of tea? I can make it the English way.'

'Did Nina teach you?'

'Nina? Why Nina?'

'Because you told me how often you stayed

with her when you were young.'

'That's true — but it was her mother who taught me, not Nina. She never had to lift a finger, bless her.'

As she moved to the door, Tessa said, 'By the way, I met her in Oslo. She's nice. Not a bit what I expected.'

Margrit halted. 'You didn't tell me.'

'I haven't seen you since that day.'

'How did you happen to meet?'

'It didn't 'happen' — I looked her up. You told me the name of the magazine she works for.'

'Did I? I don't remember.' She fiddled absentmindedly with the door knob. 'What made you look her up?'

Tessa answered evasively, 'I suppose I was curious.'

'About what?'

'About her. First Carlota and then you told me about her and both descriptions were vivid, but conflicting in a way. I suppose I wanted to find out what she was really like, and what made her leave a crippled husband.'

She thought the explanation satisfactory, but Margrit said with a hint of indignation, 'I won't let you criticise Nina. She was my friend.'

'I'm not criticising her.'

'Promise not to mention this to Lars. He has been kindness itself in having you here. It would be ungracious to upset him.'

Tessa felt vaguely annoyed by the warning, but merely answered, 'Of course I won't,' omitting to add that she devoutly hoped she wouldn't see him. So long as she was confined to this room the chance seemed remote, but before leaving his house she would have to thank him for his hospitality, and that wouldn't be enjoyable.

Margrit said briskly, 'Good. And now for that tea.' As she opened the door she looked back again. 'I'm glad you met Nina. Glad you liked her too. Did she mention me?'

When Tessa shook her head, Margrit smiled a little ruefully. 'Silly of me. I just hoped she might have enquired after an old friend.'

After the door closed, Tessa wished she had lied. It would have been worth while to make Margrit happy. She was a lonely woman, the only love in her life being her daughter, and idolising anyone as self-centred as Kerstin couldn't bring much reward.

Tessa turned her gaze back to the window. Her shoulder was tender, but free from pain, and apart from the weight of the plaster cast on her leg she felt well and rested, but the thought that she was in the Hyerdal house was disturbing. She wanted to be under no obligation to the man, or to his son, but now she was under an obligation to both; particularly to Max for rescuing her.

Snatches of memory came back again, and she remembered his arm pillowing her head as he poured sips of hot tea between her numbed lips, and the gentle way in which he did it. That had been a very different man from the one who had kissed her so violently. Which was the real Max, and would she ever know?

He had also been at her side all the way to Balestrand. She had a vague recollection of her stretcher being slid into the back of his estate car, and of his strong figure sitting beside it while the driver drove slowly over the rough fjord road. Max had held her frozen hands the whole way, imparting warmth and life into them. She remembered how reassuring they had been, giving her a feeling of safety, almost of being cherished.

And that doctor at the hospital — what had he said? 'A good thing you were found by the leader of our mountain rescue team. He not only saved your leg with that splint, but your life with his presence of mind.'

Coming back to the moment, Tessa realised that her room looked out on to a sweeping lawn which spread down to the fjord, and remembered that Hyerdal's house was long and low, projecting on stilts at this sloping end so that the whole place was on one level floor.

She wondered how soon she would be able to leave, but knew she had to resign herself to a prolonged stay. Although she felt much better she was still fairly weak, and when able to get up she would have to be taught how to walk with crutches. Hoping to escape from this house quickly was useless.

There was a sound from the door and the knob slowly revolved, followed by a shuffling noise as the door gradually opened. Tessa knew instinctively that it was Lars in his wheelchair, manipulating the door with difficulty. She was right. He propelled himself into the room, spun the chair round, closed the door, revolved the wheels again, and faced her, saying without any preliminary, 'I heard you were awake. I trust you feel better?'

'Much better, thank you.'

'You had a lucky escape.'

'Thanks to your son.'

'Partially, but thanks to your own good sense in seeking refuge in the ice tunnel. Your rucksack gave the clue — it was found not far from the entrance.'

'I had to get rid of it because the weight hindered me, and then, of course, I regretted it because it contained everything necessary to keep me alive.'

'Not everything. You had youth and good health to do that. With a burden on your back you couldn't have reached shelter. In the circumstances you did the sensible thing, but I would expect that from the daughter of an expert climber.'

'So you know.'

'Yes — Max told me. Apparently he's known for some time, but not until the night of the accident did he tell me who you were, or why he brought you here.'

'I gather there was no spare bed at the hospital.'

'That wasn't his only reason. Margrit offered to accommodate you, but my son wouldn't hear of it. I guessed the reason for his anxiety, just as I guessed your reason for visiting my studio that day.'

'You were wrong there. I didn't even know Max was your son, or where he lived, and to tell you the truth I had no particular desire to meet him again.'

Hyerdal looked sceptical at that, but all he said was, 'Nevertheless, you had a motive for that visit, and it wasn't an appreciation of art.'

'You are very astute.'

'Life has made me so.'

'But not about everything. You believe my father was your enemy. I shall never believe it, no matter what jealousy existed between you.'

He said sharply, 'And how do you know about that?'

'I — heard.'

'Village gossip, I suppose.'

She let him think that. She had to go carefully. She was surprised to hear that Lars had only learned of her identity since her arrival here. She had assumed that Max had told him long ago.

'Tell me, Miss Pickard, why *did* you visit my studio that day?'

'I hoped to find out something. I was after information.'

'From me? About what?'

'About the possible author of an anonymous letter. All I knew then was that you had lived in these parts all your life and knew everything and everybody. I thought I might get some clue which could lead me to the writer.'

'Knowing nothing of such a letter, I could have provided no clues.'

'Unless you had written it yourself.'

He rapped out angrily, 'I hated your father, and for that very reason had no desire to communicate with him.'

234

'You might have wanted to strike back.'

'I did strike back. Years ago.'

'I've heard about that. You accused him unjustly. Of that I am convinced and will always be. But as a matter of curiosity, how did you know the anonymous letter was addressed to my father?'

His mouth tilted in a wry smile. 'You can't catch me that way, girl. I knew nothing about it until Max told me the other night. He told me everything, as far as he knows it. Now I want to know more. I want to see that letter.'

Margrit brought tea at that moment. She halted on seeing Lars, and for an instant Tessa felt that she was disconcerted, but the impression passed when Margrit said lightly, 'I can't allow you to disturb my patient, Lars. If you want some tea, we can have it in the studio.'

He answered gruffly, 'I can go where I wish in my own house, can't I?'

Tessa wondered if a certain tension in the atmosphere existed only in her imagination, likewise the subtle change in Margrit's personality. She watched carefully as the woman put the tray beside her bed, fetched more pillows and banked them up, then helped her into a sitting position. The plaster cast seemed to weigh a ton.

The tray could be converted into a portable bed-table. Margrit snapped the legs open and set it in front of her. 'Eat all the toast, like a good girl,' she ordered. 'You'll be on solid foods from now on.'

Tessa recalled the woman's air of authority in the office, and realised that when undertaking a job of any kind Margrit Amundsen was a different person from the shy, diffident woman one met socially. At Nina's house in Vijne she had been the same — a woman in command, self-confident and composed. She had been like that when she walked into the room earlier, and it was emphasised now by her disapproval of Tessa having a visitor without her permission. It was startling to realise that she disliked having her authority undermined; it almost seemed as if she regarded the place as her territory.

Lars said a trifle petulantly, 'You've interrupted our conversation, Margrit.'

She smiled indulgently and took hold of the back of his wheelchair. 'That's too bad, but my patient isn't strong enough for conversation yet.'

'Nonsense — look at the girl! She's plenty strong enough — and *I*'m strong enough to manipulate my chair.'

He whirled it from the room, annoyance and frustration in every movement. Margrit raised her shoulders in a resigned shrug, like a patient wife.

'Sorry he disturbed you, dear.'

'He didn't. And he's right — I am strong enough for conversation, so please tell him to come back whenever he feels like it.'

'When *I* feel like it.' The correction was gentle. 'No visitors unless *I* say. Max put me in charge, remember.'

'I'd like to see Max. I want to thank him for rescuing me.'

'And so you shall, later on. He's away from home at the moment.'

'Away? For how long?'

'Only a short time. He went this morning, just to Stavanger. It was a surprise to me because no trip was scheduled.' She added on a confidential note, 'I suspect he has gone to join Kerstin. I know she has a few days' leave from her job. It was probably she who telephoned. He came to me right away and said he was off to Stavanger, and *was* he impatient to be! Nothing can keep those two apart.'

The door closed behind her. The toast was tasteless in Tessa's mouth, and so was the tea.

21

She didn't see Lars again, but she had visitors the next day — Dr. Vansted, who expressed satisfaction over her recovery, a physiotherapist who massaged her shoulder and left a pair of crutches, promising to return to give Tessa her first lesson the following morning, and Carlota, who brought fruit, flowers, and some clothes because she had heard from Margrit that Tessa was to be allowed up. 'And two letters from England, plus make-up to boost your morale,' she added. 'Now all you need is Kerstin to do your hair, and I've arranged that for Saturday. It will be her weekend off and she's coming to Balestrand.'

Tessa looked at her in surprise. 'Are you sure? Margrit told me she was on leave now.'

'Then Margrit's got it wrong. I was in Voss yesterday and she did my hair. That was when I fixed the appointment for you — she'll be here at eleven-thirty. Will that be all right?'

'Fine,' Tessa said thoughtfully. 'Fine . . . '

Carlota continued with a confidential air,

'Is Margrit being very managing? She can be, although one would never suspect it; when she feels at home in a place her whole personality changes. Maybe you've noticed?'

'I have a little, but why should she feel at home here?'

'Because she spends so much time in this house. She looks after Lars when Max goes away, and that's pretty frequently as you know. I told you she's over-anxious to express her appreciation, didn't I? It's this awful sense of obligation she has. By the way, Steve's outside, hoping you'll see him. Has anything gone wrong between you two? He seems positively sheepish about coming in.'

'Tell him of course I'll see him and not to be silly.'

Steve was definitely sheepish. He had brought chocolates and magazines and handed them over as if doing penance. Carlota made a great display of tact and disappeared.

'It's good of you to see me in the circumstances, Tess.'

'I think so too.'

'You haven't forgiven me for what I said about your father, have you?'

'I find it hard, but even harder to forgive you for hiding the truth all along. I liked you. I was even fond of you. I trusted you too.'

'You'll trust me again,' he said confidently,

'and *I*'m damned fond of *you*, Tess, you know that.'

His beaming self-confidence never deserted him for long. He had the resilience of a rubber ball, but instead of amusing her, Tessa found it irritating now. There had been venom in his voice when he had spoken of James and she couldn't forget it. Mistrust stirred again, and suddenly she was tired and unable to hide it.

'Want me to go?' he asked gently.

She nodded. 'Sorry, Steve.'

'That's all right, old girl.' He stooped to kiss her and she turned her head quickly so that his kiss landed on her cheek. For a moment he was nonplussed, then he patted her hand and said cheerfully, 'You'll soon be your old self again, you'll see. We'll be sailing together in no time and everything will be just the way it was before.'

She wished she could believe it. The trouble was that she still didn't know what to believe or whom to believe, and wanted desperately to see Max. If he had not gone to Stavanger to meet Kerstin he must have gone to Voss instead. There was a logical answer to everything if you looked for it. Margrit had made a mistake and, quite illogically, Tessa wanted to tell her so, if only to see her reaction. The funny thing was that when the woman appeared and Tessa told her that Carlota had arranged for Kerstin to do her hair on Saturday, all she said was, 'Good — that will pep you up, won't it? I'm glad to hear Max is bringing her back with him.'

'But not from Stavanger. She's not on leave from her job — she did Carlota's hair only yesterday.'

'Is that so? Then he must have gone to Voss to see her there. I told you they hated to be parted for long, didn't I?'

* * *

Today was Tuesday, which meant that Tessa had to wait until the weekend to thank Max for saving her life. Until then, the days spread before her like a lonely lane. She thought of him with Kerstin, and it hurt. She tried not to think of him, and that hurt too, because without him there was only emptiness.

Margrit brought her an early supper, for which she had no appetite, so she leaned back against the pillows and closed her eyes. When the door opened and Margrit came in to collect her tray, she didn't bother to open them. 'Sorry to leave it,' she murmured, 'but I'm not hungry.'

'So it seems.'

Her heart leapt and her eyes jerked open.

It was Max, looking big and solid and serious.

'Do you feel up to talking?' he asked.

She nodded mutely.

'First I want to apologise about — that night.'

'I've forgotten it,' she said quickly, knowing she never could, but the things she would remember were his ardour and his passion. He had wanted her. At least, he had wanted her.

'You mistook my motive,' he went on. 'You thought I wanted to punish you. I didn't. I wanted *you*, as I've wanted you almost since we met, and especially since that day we went climbing. I hated you, or thought I did, but you got under my skin and refused to get out of my mind.' He made a helpless gesture, a big man bewildered by something which previously he had always been able to cope with — Tessa knew that as surely as if he had told her.

'And I'm sorry for — for what I did to you before we parted. I've never struck a woman before.'

And he never would again — she knew that too.

'I told you I've forgotten that night, Max, and I want you to do the same.'

He smiled a little. 'I don't want to forget

all of it, but I do want to know that you forgive me.'

It hardly seemed necessary to say so, but because he wanted to hear it, she did, then went on, 'Far more important is what *I* want to say to *you* — thank you for rescuing me. You saved my life, I understand.'

'Thank God I was able to. I was frantic when the news went round that you were missing, and that the glacier had avalanched. It's bad enough when an unknown climber is lost. When it's someone you love, it's hell.'

She couldn't speak. They just looked at each other and she held out her arms and in one movement he was on his knees beside her bed, his face buried in her shoulder. She felt tears pricking her eyes and an unbelievable happiness in her heart. She forgot everything and everyone but this moment and themselves, until a voice said drily from the door, 'I told you I knew his reason for bringing you here, didn't I? And I wasn't wrong that day in my studio, when I said I could tell when a man and a woman were aware of each other . . . '

Tessa hastily brushed her eyes with the back of a hand, and Max kept the other in his own as he turned and looked over his shoulder. 'In some ways,' he said, 'you're a wise man, Father, but not always, and I'll prove it to you.'

'That's why I'm here,' the old man barked. 'To see that letter you told me about, and to learn more about this girl you're in love with. She's the daughter of my enemy, remember that. Daughter of the man who ruined my life. What twist of fate brought her here, in God's name, and do you expect me to bless the pair of you?'

'Whether you bless us or not makes no difference. Tessa can't be held responsible for things that are past and which you can't be sure happened, anyway. I mean that, and I'm sorry if it hurts, but injuries such as yours *could* have caused amnesia and even hallucination. Naturally you believe your version of what happened on the glacier, and I've always believed it because you did, but recently I've begun to think and reason, and to investigate similar cases in medical journals. I've talked with specialists in Oslo. What you claim to be true might be true. Then again, it might not.'

Lars said bitterly, 'A lot of things seem to have been going on behind my back. I don't take kindly to that, let me tell you. And now what about that letter? Where is it?'

Max said, 'Show it to him, darling. I know

you have it with you. It goes everywhere with you, doesn't it?'

For a brief moment Tessa wondered how he knew, because she had never told him. 'It's in the zipped pocket of my anorak. I put it there when I went climbing.' She sat bolt upright. 'My anorak! Where is it? What happened to it? *What became of my clothes*?'

'Margrit will know.' Max went to the door and called. 'The nurse did them up in a parcel and gave them to me, and I handed them over to Margrit after I brought her here to look after you.'

He was calm and confident, and so was Margrit when she appeared, although obviously surprised to see him. When asked to produce Tessa's climbing clothes, she laughed.

'Whatever for? She won't be wearing those again for months, and the trousers are a write-off anyway.'

'But not my anorak!' Tessa cried. 'I *must* have that.'

Margrit obviously considered that she had to be humoured, for she said soothingly, 'I hung them in the boiler room to dry and they're still there, safe and sound.'

Max told her to fetch the anorak and she gave a little shrug of amusement. 'I'll bring them all if it will make her happy,' she said, and went at once. In no time at all she was back with them. Tessa flung aside the tattered trousers, the chunky sweater, the loose-knit underthings, the thick climbing stockings — everything but the anorak, which she seized and unzipped the pocket.

It was empty.

They were all empty — side pockets, hip pockets, every pocket in the outfit. After frantically searching through everything, her hands fell lifelessly on to the bed. She couldn't speak.

Max asked, 'Did you go through the pockets, Margrit?'

'Of course not. Why should I?'

'To see if anything was there — anything which needed drying out, I mean.'

'I didn't think of it. Should I have done?'

'It might have occurred to you, but it doesn't matter.'

'Not matter!' Tessa sobbed. 'I came all the way to this country because of that anonymous note and now someone has taken it. I can prove nothing. Nothing!'

'But I can,' he said soothingly. 'There's a copy in my study.'

'A copy! But how did you make it? When did you get hold of it? And it won't prove anything because the handwriting will be different.'

'It can't possibly be different — it's a photostat. Two photostats, in fact; one of the letter and one of the envelope. My mother had them made when you visited her office.'

'So that was why she took them out of the room!'

Lars barked, 'What in God's name is all this about?'

'Something you've got to face up to, Father, and you'll be glad if you do. We've been wrong in some ways, you and I, and one in particular. That was why I went to Oslo yesterday, after Nina telephoned.'

Margrit tactfully began to leave the room, but Max said, 'There's no need for you to go, Margrit. After all, you're practically one of the family so there's nothing we have to hide from you. I'll be back in a moment.'

The door closed behind him.

'All the same, I must get back to the kitchen,' Margrit said. 'I've things to do.'

'What things?' Lars demanded. 'Supper's over and the washing-up machine deals with the dishes, so what in heaven's name *have* you to do? You're always on the go, Margrit. Can't you ever relax?'

She murmured something about setting breakfast trays, and then more decisively, 'The truth is that despite what Max says

I'm *not* one of the family and I don't think I should hear private matters. It would embarrass me.'

'Well, it won't embarrass us, so stay. Max seems to want you to.' The ageing voice added gently, '*I* want you to, Margrit. You're the only woman to care about me since Nina went.'

Tessa saw the deep, betraying flush on the woman's face and guessed why she had always been so anxious to show her appreciation of this man's kindness. It wasn't due to over-conscientiousness, as Carlota presumed. It was love.

But the surprise she felt was nothing compared with that which followed, for when the door reopened Max wasn't alone. His mother was with him.

Lars went rigid. Nina looked at him and said, 'I waited in Max's study. Don't be angry, Lars. It was necessary for me to come.'

'Quite apart from the fact that she wanted to,' Max added, 'which ought to mean a great deal more. That was why I brought her back with me today. The other reason was to show you these.'

He held out the photostats and his father took them unseeingly, for his eyes were still on his wife's face. His mouth quivered suddenly, then was still. He said her name in a shaken whisper. 'Nina!' Then more strongly: 'Nina — you're as lovely as ever. Lovelier, in fact.'

'If you say that again, I shall cry, Lars. Don't let me cry. Not yet.'

'When you've looked at those things, Father, I want you to look at this. Mother received it yesterday and telephoned me at once — that was why I went haring off to Oslo.' Max held out something else, and Tessa saw that it was a piece of notepaper with writing on it. 'Compare them, and you will know, as we do, who wrote the letter that killed Tessa's father.'

Lars Hyerdal's eyes left his wife reluctantly, but he had scarcely glanced at the papers before the unexpected happened. Margrit snatched them from him and turned upon Nina like a tigress

'You bitch! So that was why you wrote to me enquiring about your house for the first time in years — you wanted evidence, was that it? You wanted to compare my writing with that note! You connived with this meddlesome girl!'

'Tessa knew nothing about it. I thought I recognised the handwriting the day she showed me the letter, but wasn't sure. As you say, it's a long time since we corresponded.

You were always a mischief-maker, Margrit, and you created enough between Lars and myself to make me never want to see you or hear from you again. You poisoned his mind against me at every opportunity. You encouraged him to think the worst of James Pickard and myself, and after the accident you took advantage of his weakened physique to foster every wrong idea his sick mind seized upon, but I never imagined that even you would stoop to writing a cruel anonymous note to stab a man when he was down.'

'He deserved it, he deserved it! *Don't look at me like that, Lars . . .* '

Lars spun his wheelchair across to her and snatched the crumpled papers from her hand, and while he spread them out on his lap and studied them Max casually stationed himself by the door.

Margrit's voice rose to a scream. Tessa heard the note of desperation in it, and almost felt a pity for her.

'I did it for *you*, Lars, don't you understand? I struck at the right moment, when he was disgraced again. I saw an English newspaper at the Nordfjord Hotel one day — that young Englishman has them sent over and leaves them about. I read all about the case, how Pickard was acquitted for the death of one of his climbing pupils, and how many people blamed him nevertheless — the scandal meant the end of his school and I was glad, *glad*! It was the perfect moment to send him a reminder of past guilt, and the outcome was even better than I expected. I've always wanted to strike back for you, because he got away too lightly for what he did to you up there on the glacier . . . '

Lars held up the copy of her letter and said in an ominous voice, 'This was the most diabolical thing anyone could do. A wicked and vile thing. I despise you for it and I always will.'

'Despise me! You should be grateful — you *will* be grateful! You'll love me for it, you'll *love* me . . . ' She flung herself on her knees before him, clinging to him, pleading and triumphant at the same time. 'He killed himself — after receiving that letter, he *killed* himself! They all thought it was because of his pupil's death, but it was *I* who made him pay the final penalty and I did it for you, I hit back for *you*.'

With one out-thrust of his arm he pushed her away.

'Get her out of here, Max. Get her out of this house — and God forgive me if I ever came near to thinking the way she does.'

As Max stooped to help her to her feet she

251

sprang up and turned upon Tessa, pointing a shaking finger and unable to hide the hatred in her face. 'Damn you, Tessa Pickard. *Damn you!* Why did you have to come here and ruin everything? The moment I found out who you were I knew what had brought you.'

'How did you find out?' Tessa asked calmly. 'By searching my cabin?'

'Of course! The moment the Revolds told me your name I knew it wasn't coincidence. The papers said that Pickard left a wife and daughter, a girl named Tessa who used to go climbing with her father. Of course, I had to make sure, and I must say you made it easy for me by leaving your passport and identification papers, even your birth certificate, in an unlocked drawer. But the note was another matter. I knew you must have kept it and brought it with you, *and* why, but I never had a chance to lay my hands on it until the other day. There it was, in the pocket of your anorak, placed right into my hands!'

'So you destroyed it, but where did it get you?' Tessa turned to Nina. 'Thank you from the bottom of my heart for what you did.'

'And now, for the second time, get out of this house,' Lars ordered.

Margrit didn't even hear him. She walked

slowly towards his wife, saying venomously, '*Curse* you for what you did! All my life you've stood in my way, had the things I could never have, married the man I wanted. And what did *I* get? Your charity, your goddamned patronage — and a husband who bored me and left me badly off into the bargain. I hate you, Nina Hyerdal, and I hate this English girl too — she has stopped Kerstin from getting Max just as you have stopped me from getting Lars, and I would have got him, indeed I would! I've made myself so necessary to him since you went away that he's grown to depend on me, and once Max and Kerstin were married he would have needed me more than ever.'

'I would probably have needed you, but I would never have wanted you,' Lars barked. 'Not as a wife. Not as I want Nina whatever happened in the past.' He turned to Tessa. 'There's a penalty in every country for poison-pen writers. Do you want to bring a charge against this woman?'

'No — not now. Justice for my father, his name cleared, that is all that matters to me.'

'I'll see to that, I owe it to him. And now for the last time, Margrit Amundsen, leave my house. You can look for a job anywhere you like, but don't look to Hyerdal's for a reference.'

He spun his chair round so that his back was turned to her and he didn't speak again until Max closed the door behind her, then he said with difficulty, 'Nina — that nightmare I used to have. I still have it. I've told Max about it, but I've never told you. It is probably his reason for consulting specialists, but I can be my own psychiatrist now. That nightmare — I've begun to suspect that it isn't a nightmare at all, but the truth trying to get through to me.'

'Tell me about it,' she said gently.

'It's always the same — it always has been. I'm being carried away on a sea of ice; sometimes it is pinnacle high, mighty *séracs* threatening to fall on me, and the ice is sweeping you away too; I'm always battling through it, trying to reach you, but always the ice and James Pickard get in the way — and then the ice crashes down on me, and I wake up ice-cold and sweating. And I can never remember what went before. The nightmare starts there, and finishes the same way always.'

She stood behind his chair, slid her hands over his shoulders and said gently, 'I've often wondered if that is what happened after James left you protected, as he thought, behind a pinnacle. Your injuries were so severe that memory was blotted out.'

'Not entirely. The truth must have been there, lodged in the back of my mind, forcing itself on to me in dreams — but I wouldn't heed it.'

He seized her hands and buried his face in them.

'The other part of the truth,' she replied, 'is that I stayed with you because I *wanted* to, and I've come back for the same reason — if you will have me. No — don't say anything now. We'll talk alone.'

Max opened the door and she wheeled her husband away. After an eloquent moment Max said, 'Things will be put right — about your father, I mean. His name will be cleared, even at this late date. I know Lars. He is a just man at heart.'

'I can tell that.'

'And you — I suppose you meant to go back to England when you'd done what you wanted to do?'

'Yes.'

'And now that you have?'

'That is up to you.'

'Stay,' he commanded. 'You've got to stay — with me. I say so.'

* * *

It wasn't until later that Tessa remembered her letters. They were still on her bedside table, where Carlota had put them. She picked them up, glancing idly at the handwritings, not really interested because they represented intrusion from the outside world and she was too happily enclosed in this one, this world which was to be hers from now on and which she would share with Max. There was little room in it for anyone else and these letters, one with an English stamp and the other French, represented no more than distant voices to which she now turned an unwilling ear. The first belonged to Dan and the second to Ruth.

She opened her mother's letter first, posted from Villefranche. '*At last I am beginning to recover from the shock of your father's death and the pain he caused me . . . rest and sun and peace are doing their healing work . . . people are so kind and understanding, everyone in the hotel so friendly . . . at the casino in Cannes last night I won three thousand francs,* such *fun . . . a charming man from Nîmes took me, a restaurant proprietor . . . seems very wealthy, and so attentive, with none of that awful British reserve your father had . . .* '

Watch it, Mother, watch it! Tessa thought. A middleaged woman left comfortably off, still good-looking, ripe for flattery — a traditional target for the unscrupulous *poseur*. And a restaurant proprietor could be no more than a small café owner in France. Tessa thrust the letter back into its envelope, aware that the rest of it continued in the same vein and in no mood to read on, or to feel responsible for her mother's welfare. Ruth was old enough to look after herself and would have to learn how to do it.

Dan's letter was very different. No romantic fantasies here. '*When are you coming home?*' he demanded. '*There are things to be attended to, as you must realise. I want to go ahead with reopening the school and can't do this until we are married. Your absence is holding me up, Tessa. As soon as you return, and I insist that this must be soon, we will get married and everything can go ahead. And we must discuss this question of launching under a different name. There's no place for sentiment in business . . .* '

She thrust the letter aside impatiently, well aware that he had every intention of putting his own name to the school. It would mean the final obliteration of James Pickard, and this she wouldn't allow. She found paper and pen in a drawer beside her bed and wrote firmly: '*You must know at once that I won't be coming back, and I can't marry you, Dan. I am in love with someone else, really in love this time. I don't think this is going to disappoint you so much as losing the school, and since I won't be there to run it and I can't bear the thought of my father's dedicated work being wasted and forgotten, I've a proposition which should interest you. Under his will you inherit financially if you don't marry me, and this you deserve. It should be enough to help you to buy the school, coupled with a mortgage, and I am willing to sell to you on one condition which must be legally binding — that the name of the school remains unchanged. That is all. It must be the Pickard Climbing School permanently and for ever. You will have full control and be able to run it as you wish, and I know this will be done competently and well or my father would never have made any bequest to you. He thought highly of you as a climber, an administrator, and an instructor, and I think sufficiently highly of you as a person to entrust you with his school. But without this guarantee regarding the preservation of his name, there can be no deal.'*

She finished it with a brief and friendly message which, she knew, would pacify him. Dan was ambitious above all things, above human relationships or human emotions, the very antithesis of Max, that complex, compelling, unpredictable man whom she loved and without whom she could not live. Not an easy man. Not a conventional one. But a warm and compassionate man, and the only possible one for her.

THE END

McLEAN AT THE GOLDEN OWL
George Goodchild
Inspector McLean has resigned from Scotland Yard's CID and has opened an office in Wimpole Street. With the help of his able assistant, Tiny, he solves many crimes, including those of kidnapping, murder and poisoning.

KATE WEATHERBY
Anne Goring
Derbyshire, 1849: The Hunter family are the arrogant, powerful masters of Clough Grange. Their feuds are sparked by a generation of guilt, despair and ill-fortune. But their passions are awakened by the arrival of nineteen-year-old Kate Weatherby.

A VENETIAN RECKONING
Donna Leon
When the body of a prominent international lawyer is found in the carriage of an intercity train, Commissario Guido Brunetti begins to dig deeper into the secret lives of the once great and good.

A TASTE FOR DEATH
Peter O'Donnell

Modesty Blaise and Willie Garvin take on impossible odds in the shape of Simon Delicata, the man with a taste for death, and Swordmaster, Wenczel, in a terrifying duel. Finally, in the Sahara desert, the intrepid pair must summon every killing skill to survive.

SEVEN DAYS FROM MIDNIGHT
Rona Randall

In the Comet Theatre, London, seven people have good reason for wanting beautiful Maxine Culver out of the way. Each one has reason to fear her blackmail. But whose shadow is it that lurks in the wings, waiting to silence her once and for all?

QUEEN OF THE ELEPHANTS
Mark Shand

Mark Shand knows about the ways of elephants, but he is no match for the tiny Parbati Barua, the daughter of India's greatest expert on the Asian elephant, the late Prince of Gauripur, who taught her everything. Shand sought out Parbati to take part in a film about the plight of the wild herds today in north-east India.

THE DARKENING LEAF
Caroline Stickland

On storm-tossed Chesil Bank in 1847, the young lovers, Philobeth and Frederick, prevent wreckers mutilating the apparent corpse of a young woman. Discovering she is still alive, Frederick takes her to his grandmother's home. But the rescue is to have violent and far-reaching effects . . .

A WOMAN'S TOUCH
Emma Stirling

When Fenn went to stay on her uncle's farm in Africa, the lovely Helena Starr seemed to resent her — especially when Dr Jason Kemp agreed to Fenn helping in his bush hospital. Though it seemed Jason saw Fenn as little more than a child, her feelings for him were those of a woman.

A DEAD GIVEAWAY
Various Authors

This book offers the perfect opportunity to sample the skills of five of the finest writers of crime fiction — Clare Curzon, Gillian Linscott, Peter Lovesey, Dorothy Simpson and Margaret Yorke.

DOUBLE INDEMNITY — MURDER FOR INSURANCE
Jad Adams

This is a collection of true cases of murderers who insured their victims then killed them — or attempted to. Each tense, compelling account tells a story of cold-blooded plotting and elaborate deception.

THE PEARLS OF COROMANDEL
By Keron Bhattacharya

John Sugden, an ambitious young Oxford graduate, joins the Indian Civil Service in the early 1920s and goes to uphold the British Raj. But he falls in love with a young Hindu girl and finds his loyalties tragically divided.

WHITE HARVEST
Louis Charbonneau

Kathy McNeely, a marine biologist, sets out for Alaska to carry out important research. But when she stumbles upon an illegal ivory poaching operation that is threatening the world's walrus population, she soon realises that she will have to survive more than the harsh elements . . .

TO THE GARDEN ALONE
Eve Ebbett

Widow Frances Morley's short, happy marriage was childless, and in a succession of borders she attempts to build a substitute relationship for the husband and family she does not have. Over all hovers the shadow of the man who terrorized her childhood.

CONTRASTS
Rowan Edwards

Julia had her life beautifully planned — she was building a thriving pottery business as well as sharing her home with her friend Pippa, and having fun owning a goat. But the goat's problems brought the new local vet, Sebastian Trent, into their lives.

MY OLD MAN AND THE SEA
David and Daniel Hays

Some fathers and sons go fishing together. David and Daniel Hays decided to sail a tiny boat seventeen thousand miles to the bottom of the world and back. Together, they weave a story of travel, adventure, and difficult, sometimes terrifying, sailing.

SQUEAKY CLEAN
James Pattinson

An important attribute of a prospective candidate for the United States presidency is not to have any dirt in your background which an eager muckraker can dig up. Senator William S. Gallicauder appeared to fit the bill perfectly. But then a skeleton came rattling out of an English cupboard.

NIGHT MOVES
Alan Scholefield

It was the first case that Macrae and Silver had worked on together. Malcolm Underdown had brutally stabbed to death Edward Craig and had attempted to murder Craig's fiancée, Jane Harrison. He swore he would be back for her. Now, four years later, he has simply walked from the mental hospital. Macrae and Silver must get to him — before he gets to Jane.

GREATEST CAT STORIES
Various Authors

Each story in this collection is chosen to show the cat at its best. James Herriot relates a tale about two of his cats. Stella Whitelaw has written a very funny story about a lion. Other stories provide examples of courageous, clever and lucky cats.